If You Knew Me

Also by Anne Roiphe

If You Knew Me

A NOVEL BY

ANNE ROIPHE

LITTLE, BROWN AND COMPANY

BOSTON   TORONTO   LONDON

First Edition

This is a work of fiction. Names, characters, places, and incidents
either are the product of the author's imagination or,
if real, are used fictitiously.

Library of Congress Cataloging-in-Publication Data

Roiphe, Anne Richardson
    If you knew me : a novel / by Anne Roiphe.
        p.   cm.
    ISBN 0-316-75430-7
    I. Title.
PS3568.O53I35   1993
813'.54—dc20   92-38200

10 9 8 7 6 5 4 3 2 1

RRD-VA

*Published simultaneously in Canada
by Little, Brown & Company (Canada) Limited*

Printed in the United States of America

For my daughter Becky

If You Knew Me

THE TOWN of West Pine is only a hundred and fifty miles from the city. The ocean is clean all the way to the horizon. The summer homes were built in the early twenties, and their shingled fronts, their white porches, their brick chimneys line the dunes and the streets behind the dunes. In the estate section, huge mansions with stately columns, their long driveways bordered with roses and lilies, stand behind brick walls, behind high hedges; on the top floors are rooms for nannies and butlers. In the garages are duffel bags from boarding schools, hockey sticks, bridles, and golf bags. Once fishermen owned the small houses on the other side of the railroad tracks. Now young lawyers and advertising copywriters have moved in, with Nintendo, a VCR, a ten-speed bike. The town has restaurants with Cajun chicken and shiitake mushrooms, and the local police have become expert in stopping drunken drivers and teenagers smoking pot in the parking lots. There are still scallops in the bay. There are mussels and quahogs in the harbor. There are bluefish and tuna out at sea. There are blackberries in the brush and a riding stable behind the tennis club. There are insurance agents and dentists, landscapers with illegal aliens spraying the roses, off-season food stamps and on-season road stands selling home-baked pies. There is a bird sanctuary, an American Legion post, and three fitness centers. There are six churches filled on Sundays. The chamber music quartet plays at the Jewish Center once a month, and the Alzheimer group also meets there. In the basement of the churches the AA members serve coffee and doughnuts. Every three hours a substance abuser can find a meeting to attend if he or she wishes. The hospital is now advertising in the paper, the *West Pine Comet*, an AIDS support group in formation.

DOWN THE SHORE she saw three men at the edge of the surf, casting their lines out over the waves. Fifty yards out past the sandbar the gulls were rising and dipping, up and down, their white wings catching the flash of afternoon sun. The blues were still running. She was close enough to see the tension in the shoulders, the brace of the legs in the wet sand as the men leaned back, arched their spines, their rods bending, bobbing, with the ebb of the determined tide. The cold air was clear and dry. The September sun was already tinged with lavender but the whitecaps, rolling in from the horizon on the crest of huge waves, riding up swiftly, foam and bubble, across the damp brown sand, shone, a promise of purity, an illusion of purity. Leah knew: beneath the froth, thousands of life-forms were devouring each other, excreting, dividing, and lifting up toward the shore, away from the shore, the detritus of death, the ooze of birth. Leah, a molecular biologist now on leave, writing her articles, catching her breath, too long at the bench, reading her notes, the pages of notes, the notebooks marked and numbered, was walking on Indian Pebble Beach, stretching her legs, letting her mind drift out and back with the tide.

Midstride, awe caught her. It mingled with a joy that would not be still. Tenderness spilled over the wave chasing her ankles, tenderness for the glory of the infinite crab legs under the shifting sand, the pocked sand itself, the mound of mollusk and fish, eyeball and scale. She considered the millions of parasites that lived in the clumps of seaweed attached to the drying log ahead. Their shape and their appetites came sharply, individually to her mind: awe.

She walked, swinging her arms in her large sweatshirt, letting the salt mist sink into her skin, wet her long black hair with its few gray strands held in a silver barrette at the back of her neck. Her legs seemed set on springs; her acute eyes, perfect vision, trained for the anomaly, the detail, the shadow, flashed out, picking up the blue of mussel shell, the dried brown of seaweed, the white foam, and the padded footprints of a large dog. Now she was far from the men still casting their rods and reeling in their lines, again and again. When she looked back, they became silhouettes, apparitions, indistinct, they had no hands or heads. The gulls had moved on, farther out in the ocean, now only thin lines, scratches against the sky.

Leah saw a man walking with a woman. They were coming toward her. The man was broad and he had a wide chest. His hair was curly, his legs seemed slightly bowed. The sun glanced off the metal rim of his glasses, slashing across his face, blurring his features. He was talking loudly to the woman. She was heavy. Her hair hung in braids down her back, braids that bounced against her shoulder blades. She walked with jerks. Was she skipping or limping? She was wearing loose overalls and a red flannel shirt. The man was saying no. She was getting angry. He put his hand on her arm. She pulled away. She let out a cry. A strange cry. Maybe a whine, not a cry, angry, but not like a woman, like a cat, perhaps, whose tail has been stepped on. Was the man hurting her? Leah moved closer. The woman broke away and ran, leaning to the left, pulling a leg behind, into the surf. The water splashed up on her face. It must be cold, too cold, thought Leah. The man called out. He was forbidding the woman. He was begging her. He was following her into the water. The waves were high. They reached the woman's chest. Leah could see the outline of her full breasts. The woman threw her arms up and fell forward. The man followed. They were only a few feet from the shore, but the cold, and the tide, and the sharp slope of the shore made it hard for the man to hold on to the woman, who was larger than he. A wave came and washed his glasses off his face. Instantly they disappeared in the foam.

Leah watched. She saw the woman pushing the man away, scratching at his moving face. She saw the man pushed toward the shore by the surf and pulled to the side. Leah turned her head away. If only she had walked in the other direction. If only she didn't have to do what she knew she had to do. She hated cold water. She hated the sudden, the unexpected. She didn't want to be out there in the surf with two strangers, caught in their story. But what could she do, what else could she do? She took off her sneakers. She went into the water. Cold pulled at her legs. Christ, she hated the numbness that swept over her ankles. Christ, she hated the strangers that had made her plunge into the ocean. A wave came over her head and she ducked down, water filling her pants till they ballooned out. What had she done this for? What was the matter with her? She struggled against the lifting wave and held her balance. Cold stung through her clothes. Water ran out her nose. Water filled her ears. Christ, it was stupid. Also she was afraid. Afraid that her legs would cramp and she'd be washed out to sea. The joke was on her, a drowned Samaritan. In the upswing of a wave, the second before the downward crash, she grabbed a flailing arm. The man caught hold of the woman's other arm. The woman kept her head down but moved limply with Leah's lifting and dropping body toward the shore.

The woman hauled herself up on the sand. The man came behind. Leah stood by them, water dripping off her clothes, cold air numbing her skin. The woman smiled, a vague smile like a child offering you tea from an imaginary cup. The man patted her broad shoulder. The woman's overalls were covered with wet sand. There was sand in her hair, water spilled from her shoes. She spit sand out of her mouth. "Thank you," said the man to Leah. The spray from the pounding waves swept around them. The man's lips were blue.

That was how they met. Ollie Marcus, English teacher, and Leah Rose, and Ollie's sister, Sally. There was something wrong with Sally. It was clear to Leah as they walked back up the beach to the parking lot. The woman shook her wet head like a dog after a swim. Her braids lashed from side to side. She stopped to pick up a large empty clamshell. She not only limped but one arm seemed to hang useless at her side. Her face was round and smooth. There was a small space between her front teeth. Her eyes were large and blue but they seemed crooked in her face. They moved too suddenly or remained too still. Her tongue moved forward and back in her mouth, appearing suddenly between her lips. Time had rolled over her without stripping away childhood, without adding shape. Her breasts, her hips, now seemed invisible, covered in flesh, covered by the wet of her overalls.

"You must be cold, Sally," said Ollie. Sally said nothing. "She has moods," said Ollie to Leah. Leah pushed her feet, now covered with damp sand, into her sneakers. Ollie shivered. In the parking lot he helped his sister into their Dodge pickup truck.

"Do you need a lift?" he asked.

"No," said Leah, "I'm staying at our family house, just

down the road." The sun was sliding down. Orange streaks crossed the dunes, rust stains on the high cattails that lined the bluff. A clear white light flickered under the branches of the rosebushes. Leah was leaning forward, taking off her wet sweatshirt and wringing it out.

Ollie said, "Is your husband with you?"

"I have no husband," said Leah. Divorced, he thought. "I never married," she said. She turned her head away and began to walk with a quick stride, her wet pants clinging to her legs. She held her dripping sweatshirt in one hand carefully away from her body.

"It's near suppertime," said Ollie to his sister as he climbed up into the cab. "French toast with sugar," he said to her. He felt the cold wool of his shirt on his chest. He saw the pools of water and the dark sand on the rubber mat under his feet. His hair was now flat to his head. There were pinch marks on the sides of his nose where his glasses had rested. He softly smiled, a half smile, at his sister, a tired smile, a touch of irony, a brush of patience, a tidal wave of gentleness. As he turned on the motor the radio began, Patsy Cline walking around after midnight. Sally bobbed in rhythm. He drove slowly. Without his glasses the side of the road wavered and the trees ahead seemed dwarfed and the curves changed their shape as he approached them.

Leah opened the door to the house and, feeling cold, stood in the hall and stripped off all her wet clothes. There was a dark mole on her collarbone and a sprinkling of freckles around her hips. There was a red mark on her waist where the belt of her jeans had cut into the flesh. Her eyes were large, alert, brown. Brown like the forest floor, her father had said.

She didn't look at her body in the mirror that faced her at

the top of the stairs. Her body was a shell, a blending, bending structure, warped and eased by weather like the gray barns with abandoned cars in front that marked the route to the highway back to the city. She didn't notice her face, which in fact flashed with quick light, a knowing, wondering, doubting look, a sorrowing tender look, an I-won't, I-can't, I-might look, one that had been with her since childhood, one that showed in all the pictures, graduating from kindergarten, playing ball, holding the hand of her stooped gray father. This look, her look, sloped across her high cheekbones, down her long oval face, and splashed across her lips, curled in the muscles around her mouth, a mouth that was not bitter, not harsh, not unkind, not indifferent, not young, definitely not young, but not old either. She was a measurer, a weigher, a counter of probability, but also a dreamer, a person with unlimited hope; expectations, although kept under guard, undimmed. Sometimes when she was concentrating hard she bit at the underside of her bottom lip. In the shower she let the hot steam fall over her, soak through her scalp and beat against her spine.

Leah Rose, wrapped in a flannel bathrobe, her legs stretched out bare beneath her, turned the channels of the TV till she found a weather report. She watched the map with its satellite swirls of cold fronts, the neat waves of pastels indicating pressure levels, moving fronts, rain expected, and estimated temperatures. She listened to the cheerful well-groomed young lady with a pointer describe the atmospheric movements expected in the next twenty-four hours. She always watched the weather reports, in the morning, in the late afternoon, at night. She preferred the national reports, or perhaps the global reports, the humidity in Paris, the potential storm over Kyoto. In the newspaper she read it again. The heat in India, the expected snow flurries in Colorado.

She ate her supper at the table in the kitchen, an eggplant salad she had prepared the day before, a roll, and a glass of milk. She was healthy, health showed in the gloss of her skin, in the thick dark patina of her hair, in the quick lifting of her arms and the tense muscles of her calves. She avoided foolish risks, unlike Boris, her postdoc lab assistant, who smoked out on the balcony at the end of the hall, coming back into the lab with the smell of nicotine in his hair. He told her wonderful jokes, dirty jokes that made her laugh, shyly the laugh would jump into her throat and sneak out, a burble, a giggle, a joyous rumble, a blush rising from the neck to the forehead. She would laugh even when she wasn't sure, absolutely sure, she understood the joke. He told her stories about his girlfriend who wanted a big ring when he could only afford a little one. Leah smiled. "Don't smoke," she said to him.

"I can't help it," he said.

"Use your head," Leah said.

"In my head is this idea I need a cigarette," he said.

"All right," said Leah. People are not programmed like bacteria, for survival. Too bad. Leah stopped thinking about her lab assistant's smoking. She concentrated on his girlfriend. "Get the ring," she said. "Don't be small."

"I'm not small," he said. "I'm broke."

"I'll lend it to you," said Leah. "I have money in the bank." She did. She did not need all the salary the institute gave her. She did not need all the funds that her father and mother had left her, their only child. She gave money to the Gay Men's Health Collective, to the Southern Poverty Law Center, to the home for the deaf and the aged, to the

Barnard Alumna Fund, but mostly she gave to children's diseases, cystic fibrosis, spina bifida, cerebral palsy, leukemia. The envelopes came, every day more and more. She opened them, read them, stared at the pictures of doe-eyed children whose futures were clouded.

She had few wants, few wants that she could name. She had no desire for more clothes; her lab coat covered most everything. She had no need for travel or cars or jewels. She had no time to learn about the brand names of furniture or sheets. She was occupied in the pursuit of molecular matter, chromosomes. RNA binding to DNA, that behaved or did not behave in radioactive solutions that would strip away the confusions and explain, might explain the bumping together of cell and surface, nucleus and drifting chemical, receptors singing their siren songs to passing molecules. Proteins and acids, there was the soup of the divine. Other researchers also had desires for pâté and champagne, for dancing and sex, for walks under palm trees or sojourns in foreign cities. Leah was single-minded and perhaps in mixed company moderately shy. She was not indifferent. If anything, she suffered from wanting too much. She wanted her experiments to work without hitch, the numbers to come clear into patterns, the truth, the tiny, once obscure, now obvious corner of the truth that would show itself beneath her microscope, fixed with shining solutions, southern blot, northern blot, photograph like a gleaming planet, that truth for which she would wait patiently, eyes focused, mind poring over the lists, the numbers, that truth which perhaps meant nothing, led to nothing, promised nothing, that truth was what she wanted, would consider her rightful portion, would bend her head in gratitude if it came to her, satisfying the thing within her that made her bite her nails down to the cuticles, sometimes at night pull at the left side of her long hair till a few strands would wind themselves around her fingers and her scalp would hurt.

It was childish to think about it, and Leah didn't, hardly ever, not since the first days of graduate school, but behind her concern with the dividing pulsing stuff inside the test tube, the movement or lack of it on the slide she held precisely between thumb and forefinger, lay a great storm, a boiling fury at the things that corrupted and misfired, grew too much or too little, blew molecules apart and turned human biology into a travesty, a train falling off the tracks. The thing might start as an invisible spot of protein, a molecule of hemoglobin, carrying false instructions from a traitor neuron, in a gallbladder, a spleen, the spine, the cortex, the deepest of bone marrow, the tiniest of fetal cells, sending crazy messages through the placenta, through the womb, riding on the tip of an otherwise normal helix and become, how many cell generations later, the cruel, hideous, Byzantine mask of death. She knew it. She hated it. "Great White Hunter," she called herself. "Memsahib," she would mutter when she put in an order for more beakers. She had no patience for antivivisectionists. She could grab a hamster by the neck and find its vein or slash the throat of a mouse while ordering her lunch. She could program machines with her eyes closed, though she didn't. "Rock and roll," she would say when the results were as expected. She moved quickly and kept careful notes. She had ambitions to repair the irreparable.

She relaxed sometimes. She went to the Museum of Natural History. She went there almost every week. She liked the fossils. She knew the names of all the bones. She adored the dinosaurs. She often found herself standing in a group of six-year-olds and their teacher staring up at the huge jawbones, the vertebrae of the *Tyrannosaurus rex*. Monster yes, but what a grand thing, what a design. In her ears she heard his thumping steps over the wild growth, the rocky ledges of earth. She liked the lit display cases with tigers and kangaroos and scenes of far-off African veldts, where the creatures were frozen in action, permanently caught between killing and being killed. She liked the white tiger that peered out behind the glass, looking for prey. She liked the huge whale that hung from the ceiling and the way you could walk around him on the balcony, locating the blowhole, looking at the dark skin that shone from lacquer and paint. She liked the lizards and the eggs and the birds' nests. She liked the flow of children, with name tags and lunch boxes, moving through the halls. Of all the museums she had been in, this was the one that made her want to spend the night. This was the one whose membership card she carried with her at all times. She was grateful to the trustees of the museum, the anthropologists and natural scientists who had with determination built the museum in a city devoted otherwise to the pursuits of the profane. She would sit, till the guard would chase her, at the base of the elephant statue in the large dark room on the first floor and feel delight, great delight. She would let time flow over her, not the hour of her lunch but the eons of evolution. It brought her peace. What if Darwin had not been born? He had.

Now she curled her legs under her and stretched her back up straight so that in the glowing light of the television she appeared to be a Gauguin model, slightly green, mysterious, waiting, poised on the brink of knowledge, hardened by necessity but still with a running in the nerves, like an underground river, pouring, rushing forward.

*   *   *

Later, after the last weather report, she climbed into bed, the same bed she had slept in as a child when her parents vacationed by the sea. They were gone. The house was hers. In the dark she could hear the ocean over the dunes, nibbling at the sand, foaming up, sliding back. Her window overlooked the small garden, grass turned brown from the heavy heat of summer, and the last leaves hung brittle from the trees, and the evergreen at the edge of the driveway swayed in the gentle sea wind. She could smell the salt and the brine. Seaweed, poppers and fern, crab-ridden, scallop-hiding seaweed drifted upward with the tide. The stars were hidden by clouds. The horizon slipped backward into blackness. Offshore the night spread.

She could see the moon, now a thin crescent covered moment to moment by passing clouds. Her doll's house was still in the corner. Her mother and father, whispering in the hall, that she could only remember. Remembering, she fell asleep.

In the early hours of the morning. A pair of glasses, one side of the frame twisted, washed up near the lighthouse twenty miles away from where Ollie Marcus had lost them. He was using his second pair, reading *Moby Dick*. He read it again each fall before teaching it to the senior class. He read it the way a man touches a woman he has been married to for thirty years. The excitement is muted but the pleasure is there, enhanced with memory, ripened with repetition, needing no attention but necessary all the same. His sister was sleeping deep and quiet, far away her body drifted in place on her bed. He had pulled up the covers that had slipped to the floor. He had left on the night-light so that if she woke she would immediately see the familiar room. He had forgotten to put her wet clothes in the dryer. They stayed on the floor. Above them hovered the smell of salt and sea.

Ollie Marcus and his sister lived in the house they had been raised in, a small dark Victorian not far from the railroad tracks, right behind the long-closed store. The rusted sign, Marcus Hardware, Paints and Parts, sat in the shed behind the house. The brown shingles on the store's roof had fallen off in patches. The walls were leaning in. The door was locked, the front window boarded. The Village Improvement Society was always after Ollie to tear the store building down. He hadn't yet but one day he would, he promised them.

More than a half century before, Solomon Marcus and his wife, Miriam, eager to begin the story of their lives, driven by the winds of Depression, driven by expectation that sea air would lead to profits, by Solomon Marcus's theory that a town without a hardware store was a town about to prosper, took their young marriage and all their savings and borrowing from relatives, and came to West Pine just as Hitler marched into Poland.

As a child, Oliver had sat in the back of the store and eaten his lunch on the checkered oilcloth that covered the little table his mother had set for him. He smelled the lumber in the backyard. He smelled the soap his mother used to clean the floor. He smelled the glue and the paint and the rubber mats on the shelves. He listened in the darkened corner for the sounds of customers coming and going. He memorized the names of screws and picture hooks and gardening gloves. In the evening after the store was closed, his mother and father would sit in the living room and count the day's receipts. Then they would lean against each other on the stuffed couch and Oliver would hear them, his mother's rippling laugh, his father's echoing growl, a gasp, a breathing hiss, "Oh, oh," "Not now, not here," "Oh," "Oo, um," and he would make a noise, maybe like an airplane, so they would know he was really there and did not like to be forgotten. Later when he was in school and he read all the time, after his sister, Sally, was born and his mother was sewing her dresses and brushing her daughter's thick brown hair and his father was coming in and picking up his second child and saying "She's the best thing that ever happened to me," and Oliver had already gotten glasses and learned what it was to be American and to say the Pledge of Allegiance and to make Christmas decorations in school, later when the television played in wavy lines and his father was laughing, he would take a book down to the cellar and under a bare light bulb turn the pages. He needed a place to get away.

Leah Rose had decided to take a sabbatical, a year away from her lab. The work was stalled. Leah admitted it. Her ideas were stale. Her mind was not sparking, not driving forward. She was circling around and around. This happened. This was not surprising. It was hard but not unexpected. The work, benchwork, was not supposed to, not expected to, not likely to move forward at a steady pace. Only beginners thought of science as a path always leading forward. Anyone who had worked in a lab understood that there were gambles and failures and dry times. Leah wasn't panicked but she was bored. She bored herself. She did not love herself. Why should she? Yes, she had burnout. Yes, she forgot to say good morning to her doorman, forgot her Guarneri concert at the Y, fell asleep during a play about Irish terrorists. She slept right through the mock explosion and the dry-ice fog blowing over the heads of the audience. Her old college roommate who lived in New Jersey with her husband and three children and two Labradors had said to her, "You need a change, you need to rest. Go on a cruise. A lot of single women your age take cruises and who knows." Leah didn't want whatever it was that happened on a cruise. If she had wanted that she would have found it years ago. "Put an ad in the personals," said her friend. "Professional woman, scientist, forty-one years old, wants companion, interested in fossils, nonsmoking."

"Ugh," said Leah.

"I know you like your science exact," said her friend Myrna, who illustrated children's books and lived in the Village with her third husband, Richard, and his daughter, Sheila, from a former marriage, and her son, Danny, from her second marriage, who kept snakes for pets and fed them live mice, which Leah, who was used to mice, found not as disgusting as most. Her friend Myrna said, "Why don't you try therapy? A woman your age, after all, must have reasons for avoiding men, you've avoided long enough. Maybe now is the time. Go see my shrink."

"No," said Leah, "I don't need a therapist. I need a vacation. There's nothing wrong with my mind."

"You're lucky," said Myrna, "or you're lying."

"Myrna," said Leah. "I'm just going through a bad time."

"Oh, yeah," said Myrna. "That's what you tell yourself?"

"Myrna, I'm going to hang up on you. You're the most annoying friend I have."

"You're probably right," said Myrna.

"My problems are banal, boring," said Leah.

"That's the worst kind," said Myrna.

"Oh, for God's sake," said Leah.

"I think you're sad," said Myrna. "I think you need somebody to curl up against at night. I think you spend too much time in the Museum of Natural History, though Danny appreciated your taking him last week. I think your affection for old bones is weird. Can you name me one other grown woman in America who has a dinosaur poster on her bathroom wall? In fact, you're wasting away, some part of you, that is. After all, you have the sex life of a panda. I think they do it once every five years."

Leah said, "Please, stop it."

"All right," said Myrna.

Dr. Grossman, who ran the lab, the oncogene expert, the one who went to the meetings and came back with the latest ideas, whose name appeared at the top of Leah's papers, said one day, "Leah, I think you should take some time off. Something is bothering you."

"Nothing is bothering me," said Leah. "I'm just getting older."

"Happens to us all," said Dr. Grossman, who thought of Leah as a single rose in a thin glass vase, drooping, dropping petals. "Go to Florence," said Dr. Grossman, "the Italian air will do you good." Dr. Grossman collected drawings from the Italian Quattrocento.

"Have you considered a woman," said another friend, who was a musicologist, an old roommate from college who had discovered her true sexual nature in her senior year and had announced that women who desired other women were purer of heart, unsullied by alien substances, kept their girlhood forever, and would never be subject to unreasonable domination. "A woman in your bed," said her friend, "might wake you up."

Leah laughed. "If I'd wanted a woman," said Leah, "you and I, long ago, wouldn't we have?"

"We would," agreed her friend. "But I could introduce you, a young one, a student perhaps, almost a boy, so flat-chested."

"No," said Leah. "I don't want someone else in my bed. I need to rest."

"Someone else in the bed, that's how most of us rest," said her friend. Leah considered.

"Not me," she said.

"A woman," said her friend, "a woman with no bad habits."

"No," said Leah. "Don't pity me," she said to her friend.

"I do," said her friend, "I do." Which is why Leah decided to take the year, the academic year, away from the postdocs, the graduate students, the Friday-afternoon conferences, the work: even to give up her afternoons in the museum. Inspiration had come to the chemist Kekule in a dream. He had seen a snake eating its tail and understood the molecular structure of the benzene ring. Inspiration had come to Dr. Bob Weinberg while crossing the Charles on a bridge in a snowstorm. Inspiration had once come to Dr. Grossman while floating in the bathtub of a Holiday Inn in Waco, Texas. Why shouldn't she walk along the beach, listen to the ocean, and drift?

It would perhaps have been better to rent a house somewhere else. This one had the stale smell of old summers. She found her book on shells from around the world, the one she had been given for her tenth birthday by her father. There it was in his round European handwriting, flourishing and looping across the page, "To Leah," it said, "who appreciates." Did I appreciate it enough? she wondered. Did her father know that she spent hours memorizing the names, making drawings of her favorites, considering the shapes and eating habits of the creatures who had once dwelled inside the corkscrews, the huts, the flat scalloped mineral that was pink, or beige, blue, or white, buffeted across coral or sea grass, buried in the sandy bottoms, or cresting in the foam? Looking at the book now, Leah breathed deeply. Only children missed their fathers. Only children waited at the window for the familiar shape, the known voice to appear. Only children who could embrace the knees or lie against the shoulder, or lean on the arm of a chair, only children had holes in them that filled up when their fathers came home. In the few weeks since she had come, unpacking her Nissan, carrying in her computer, her tapes, her books, her heavy sweaters, and her Mozart CDs, she had twice heard a noise in the kitchen and thought it was an intruder. Once she went into the bathroom and locked the door. It was nothing. It was her imagination. Leah admitted that traces of the old summers in the house — with the smell of mold in the closet where she had once left her wet bathing suit too long on a pair of sneakers, with the sound of German running like an open tap through the living room — were hanging about, were hard to erase. She ached when she woke in the morning. Perhaps her childhood mattress was no longer adequate. Perhaps she was sleeping strangely. Her neck felt stiff. To cure it she did yoga exercises. She caught a glimpse of herself in the mirror, a long-faced woman, hair escaping her clip, with sweat dripping down the backs of her ears. She was not, she would not allow it, there was no excuse for it: she was not lonely.

Leah sat down at her desk and looked at her material, her tabulations, her calculations. The problem of the precise protein that was needed to stop the cell from dividing, to start the cell dividing, this was her work. Her mind would wander. She would fix herself coffee. She would go up the stairs and down the stairs, sliding her hand along the banister. She called Myrna in Greenwich Village. Myrna talked. Sheila, her stepdaughter, would not look her in the eye, walked out of the room when she appeared. A gold circle pin was missing. Had her stepdaughter taken it? Her son, Danny, the one with the snake, was teasing girls in school. The teacher had sent a note. His work was erratic. His attention span is on a downward curve, said the note. Her husband was thinking of buying a gun. Every night he brought home another Clint Eastwood movie. "Is that normal in a real estate lawyer?" Myrna asked. "Sheila whispers about me into the telephone. I can't make out what she's saying." Leah listened.

"Come visit me," said Leah. "We could walk on the beach."

"Someday," said her friend.

"What if I really need you?" said Leah.

"I'll come," said Myrna.

"Not yet," said Leah.

After the phone call Leah took the car to town. On the way she passed the Senior Citizens' Center. A poster in the window said Save the Indian Burial Ground. The senior citizens were against disturbing the dead. A consortium of developers was for it. An attendant was helping an old woman out of a van. She pushed her walker ahead of her. My mother could have been that old, Leah thought. She considered longevity. I might have forty more years. Still enough time to get to the promised land.

In town Leah went to the drugstore. She bought a bar of rosemary soap and apricot shampoo. Ollie Marcus, standing in line, turned and saw Leah behind him. There was a dark anxious look in her eyes, a space around her. She was

standing close to him and yet she seemed far away. Ollie
was stirred. He had learned to ignore that stirring. A man
could not act like a squirrel, running up trees satisfying every twitch of hormone, every rising of gland. He was a
teacher who watched legs and full young breasts, breasts
that grew before his eyes, and the bending of the naked arm
and the swing of the rounded backside going down halls.
He ignored stirrings. Not all through the night, of course.
Dreams were beyond his control. In dreams he sometimes
saw things that embarrassed him in the mornings. Also in
dreams he often fell off ladders, down bluffs, into ravines,
beds of nails, ditches, into the town dump, where he would
lie powerless to move as the bulldozers approached, pushing ahead mounds of empty orange juice containers,
chicken bones, and sanitary napkins. In that dream the sea
gulls that perched on the hills of dirt above the ravines
squealed and called to each other, a sound that would echo
in Ollie's ears long after he had awoken.

Now he saw Leah. Leah saw him. She noticed that behind his glasses, his eyes were the ghost blue of early morning. His nose was wide and his face was broad. Like a Saint
Bernard in the snow roaming the mountains for victims of
an avalanche, he had a gentle but determined look. She noticed that he was shifting his weight from foot to foot, impa-
tience, awkwardness, she wasn't sure. She noticed that his
ears were not pressed flat to his head. She noticed that his
hair was unruly, gray in the front, curly, thick. She thought
of touching his hair. The thought surprised her. She looked
away. She looked back. He was smiling at her, sort of smiling, a softness in the cheek, a tilt of the head, a kind of
shuffle of the feet. He recognized her. Shyness made her
bend her head down. Curiosity brought it up. He took a
step toward her. She froze in place. He was carrying his

briefcase. She saw, stuffed in the side pocket, *Moby Dick*, a well-thumbed copy, little notes sticking up between the pages. "I read *Moby Dick*," she said, "in high school."

"Did you like it?" he asked.

She tried to remember and shrugged.

"If I had taught you, you would have liked it," he said.

"Would I?" she said.

"Yes," he said because he believed it to be true. "Were you all right, the other day? It was cold, too cold for a swim." He moved closer to her. She took a step backward.

She nodded. "I'm all right."

"Good," he said. There was silence.

Ollie paid for his athlete's foot medication. It never went away, the fungus between his toes. It got worse or better. It was his lifetime companion.

That night Ollie Marcus fixed dinner, spaghetti and meatballs. He sang a favorite of Sally's, "Mister Rogers' Neighborhood." His voice was deep and rocking, lilting, suggesting that everything in the neighborhood was tied up, secured, would rest well, would be fine, would not change, would not make sudden motions, would last forever, just as it was. Sally sat in her chair and waited for dinner. She sang along with her brother. In the other room the TV news went on. On his desk Ollie's class book and his papers waited for his attention. The dark was coming earlier and earlier. The brittle leaves of the oak that stood in the yard had not yet turned but their color was flat. Some had slipped from their branches as the wind from the sea rattled the panes. There was a drawing on the wall. Ollie had bought it himself at a yard sale. It was a charcoal print of a woman standing in a bath in a tub. Her towel had fallen to the floor. The woman was tall and her hips were wide.

Tonight he felt peaceful, even hopeful. He thought it odd how the smell of meatballs, the open jar of supermarket sauce, the sound of the familiar tune, the hum of the news, could arouse in a man an interest in knowing what would happen next.

Back at Barnard when Leah had been a young scientist, attracting the attention of the older professors who would arrange summer internships for her in labs at Bar Harbor, Cold Springs, she had taken a modern dance class to fulfill her gym requirement. Project your image against the far wall, the teacher said, jump toward it, join it. Move to join it. She had jumped, leapt across the floor, and in a moment of peculiar exhilaration felt herself coming close to her imaginary self on the far wall. She had bent her arms as she was told and she danced a poem of Wallace Stevens about blackbirds, she moved in her leotard back and forth and waved her arms up and down. She felt silly. She sweated dark circles under her arms. When they performed in the gym for the alumnae reunion she wore a green leotard. She was a vine climbing on the tower. Another girl was Rapunzel letting down her hair. The room was still. The lights flickered across her body. She felt her skin glow and her mind floated off, leaving her body in unaccustomed amazement. Now in her house she put on an old recording of *Peter and the Wolf.* Years ago her father had taken her to see a performance at City Center. She stretched out her arms and her legs and in the privacy of her living room she bent over and back, she was the wind with the flutes, she was the wolf with the French horns, she was the violins trilling danger as she rushed from one side of her living room to the other. Thank God, she thought, no one can see me. Thank God I live alone. But she didn't mean that. She just meant that her

bare feet on the floor stamping to the music reminded her
that once she had been a vine climbing a tower.

Leah found a sea gull stumbling about in her garden. The
bird had squalled angrily at her as she reached down to pick
him up. He flapped his wings but stayed on the ground. He
moved in double time, with a sideways crossover walk like a
vaudevillian getting off the stage. He listed to the left, he
dragged his belly through the grass. She took a towel and
swooped him up. "Hold on, Groucho," she said to him as
she drove with one hand, keeping the other on the firmly
wrapped bird.

Ollie and Sally were at the vet's with their cat, Elijah, a
calico of enormous size, whose green eyes were running
with pus. Sally had a cold. Her nose was red and swollen.
Many of Ollie's students were home sick. Some were just
pretending. It was understandable. It was Indian summer
and the warmth came through the windows, sat on the
shoulders of the boys and girls, and made their heads loll.

Sally fidgeted in the chair, which was too small for
her. Her bottom hung out over the edge. She sneezed on the
cat. Ollie leaned over and, taking a tissue from his jacket
pocket, wiped up the mucus, off the cat fur, off Sally's arm.
The vet was late. Leah saw Ollie and shyness swept over
her. The sides of Ollie's chest squeezed together. The air
around Leah seemed to vibrate. Her hair fell forward over
her face. Ollie leaned out in his seat. He wanted to see her
eyes. He wanted her to see him looking. Leah shifted in her
seat. She knew he was looking. She felt taut, a fullness in
the abdomen that sank down into her thighs. When had
that happened to her last? She tried to remember. She
waited till she thought he must have turned away. She lifted
her head and found herself staring straight into his face. His

eyes behind the glasses blinked, moist, soft, interested, lit with the mind behind. She leaned a little forward over her bird. The bird screamed its frantic caw. The cat rattled something deep in its throat. Sally grabbed the cat's fur. "Gentle," said Ollie, to his sister. But his eyes were on Leah. Sally coughed.

The vet taped the gull's beak together, picked up the wing, dangled the orange legs, all the while the heart of the bird beat in panic, the feathers rose and fell in rapid motion on its breast. "Do you want me to kill it?" he asked.

The vet sprayed the table with an antiseptic. The bird was in a cage. Its black eyes were hard as pebbles. Waste of time. Leah was embarrassed. Grief followed. She turned her head away so the vet wouldn't see her flash of sorrow.

"We find them all the time with fishhooks in them, sardine cans, pacifiers," said the vet. Leah nodded.

" 'Bye, Groucho," she said.

On the way out Leah turned and smiled quickly at Ollie and he saw a blood-colored wave cross her face, a mottling of skin that made him grasp the arm of his chair and hold on. Somewhere into the spinal fluid, adrenaline, the hormone for fight and flight, released itself into his bloodstream. He was a disciplined man, not a boy or a child or a beast in the jungle that consumes and eliminates, heats up and releases itself at a whim. Nevertheless, he followed Leah out to the parking lot. He wanted to say something intelligent, winning, sophisticated. He said, "Sorry about your gull."

"Don't be," she said. "Some clam lives because this gull dies."

"Hell," said Ollie. He laughed, a deep big belly laugh. "Tough lady," he said to Leah.

"Maybe," she said and shyly turned her head away.

He stood there, stupidly. His eyes followed her car till it disappeared from view. He was, though he told himself he was not, interested.

Back in her kitchen a humming sound was in her head, it said, I'm hungry, I'm thirsty, I'll stop at the store and buy something good to eat. I'll put on some Mozart and I'll take a shower and wash my hair. The hum also mentioned taking a look at the sunset at the bay and reading *Moby Dick* again. Maybe she would like it this time.

Leah had a phone call from Boris. The lab was quiet without her. "Like death," he said. "I'm bored," he said. "Come back."

"I'm resting," she said.

"From what?" he asked.

"I'll be back," she said.

"When?" he asked.

She said, "There's a fog here today. Everything is wet, my hair is wet, my shoes are wet. I can't see but a few feet ahead of me."

"Grossman has me splicing fourteen hours a day," said Boris.

"Do you like modern dance?" asked Leah.

"Where they leap around near-naked and moan on the stage pretending to be leaves falling off a tree?"

"Yes, that," said Leah.

"I can take or leave it," said Boris.

God, how Leah loved the fog. When she was a child she had walked in it on the beach in the summer, early, before everyone else was awake. She had let the salt wetness soak into her skin and through her shorts. Once, just as her body was changing and she was growing so fast that her dungarees were inches above her ankles, she had a friend from school down for the weekend. The friend had been afraid as the mist rolled over them, what if someone comes to get us, what if we stumble on a dead body? Leah had laughed. She wasn't afraid of bodies or things covered by mist. The salt air went deep into her lungs. Everything had its cause, its reasons. There was a purpose in the global running of tide and the spin of the earth on its axis. Understanding was all she wanted. Leah would run at the water's edge in the fog when the ocean was wild, the spray would hit her face and sting, the sound of the sea would orient her, right and left. Sometimes she stumbled on a log or a broken clamshell or a buoy washed overboard from a passing fisherman's boat. It didn't matter. She put her hand in her friend's hand and she led her along the shore.

"See," she said, "it's all right."

"Will you always be my friend?" her friend had asked.

"I don't know," said Leah, who was old enough by then to understand that friendships, like other clusters of life-forms, rearrange themselves according to pulls and pushes beyond her control. "But I want to be." Leah had admired her friend's mother, who wore hats with flowers in the brim and read romance novels and sang songs, accompanying herself on the piano. Leah watched other people's mothers for clues to alternate possibilities. The girls had built a castle of sand, with many rooms, and they had discussed the future of the castle, the landscaping of the grounds. Leah's friend had wanted a ballroom to invite boys to a dance. Leah wanted a shell collection and an observatory to watch the stars. The girls had stayed at the beach till Leah's father had come to find them. Leah's friend had wanted to build a moat to protect their castle from the tide. Leah had smiled. It can't be done, she explained. "Let it go."

Ollie said to his honors class, "Close your eyes, feel the boat rolling in the waves, feel the spray in your face, feel the water at your feet hitting the deck and sliding toward you. Think of the whale deep below. Feel the whale deep below." Martha Stimmer gasped. Ollie stopped. He looked out the window. The fog was heavy. The train whistle blew. Bruce Holloway kicked the chair in front of him. Ollie wheeled around. "What is it you want, what do you want badly enough to chase it across the ocean, what are you hunting? I want to hear, two hundred words from each of you for Friday morning." There was a groan. Too soon for a paper. There was a sound of slamming books and shuffling feet and the pitch of conversations, not for him, not to him, the conversations pushed out the door and faded down the hall. Ollie leaned against the sill. He felt the schoolroom lurch forward, the ocean roil, the whale underneath. He leaned his head against the windowpane. His own theatrics embarrassed him. His mother had said, "Don't exaggerate, don't lie, don't make trouble. Don't take every little thing so hard. Don't make such a big deal. What's so special? You're so different? You want everybody should look at you? Be quiet." He had tried. He did try.

"How's it going?" Lydia Hamilton, who had never learned how to keep mayhem out of her math class, asked as she caught up with him in the hall.

"Ah, the little minds are open, waiting for my words, just as always," said Ollie.

"Really," said Lydia, who could never tell if her leg was being pulled until it came off entirely. It was a terrible handicap, socially speaking.

"No," said Ollie. "Not really." But he smiled broadly so he confused her again. He smiled because he thought of them at the brink there, not having yet done any harm, pimpled and plump girls, boys with muscles ripping across still-skinny chests, knowing nothing and everything, wise somehow, why were they so wise, already expecting rough times, planning to go off, out of town, and conquer, or planning to stay, perennials blooming in their folks' garden. They didn't have to be told that under every rock things were crawling. They had their secrets. Each was terrified of being left out, found out, passed over. Was that Holloway kid taking something? Ollie's heavy eyebrows curled together as he considered how he'd knock the kid's head off if he found him in the parking lot down by the beach putting something into his mouth that would shrink his already not so brilliant brain cells. His chest heaved with a deep breath, inhale, exhale. Inside the school his kids were safe from everything but each other. Outside the school they were safe from nothing. Each Friday afternoon he ended all his classes with the statement "Don't die over the weekend." "Don't worry," they said to him. "Be cool, man," they said to him. "Don't drink and drive," he would say. "Sure," they said. The girls giggled. They were like clowns packed in the circus car, pleasure-seekers, understanding love and death but nothing in between, riding the rough seas with a bathtub for a boat and an umbrella for an oar, and he was the landlocked customs officer, the insurance agent who kept accounts.

Before June he would amaze them with the meaning of simile and teach them to honor their own stories. That's what he'd do. He always did. He would get calls in the night, boys who had questions they couldn't put into words. He found the words for them. Girls who had been betrayed, betrayal was everywhere. He held them with his voice, laughed at them till they laughed too. They trusted him, sometimes not far enough, not in time. Only the names of the bands changed, only the names of the drugs changed, the plots were the same as each child pressed against him, new, irregular, warm, unusual. "You're a fool if you fall in love with death," he said each fall. "I hate fools," he said in case they hadn't heard. It surprised Ollie how he could still hold every face separate, clear, sharp, a repository of his hope, a reflection of his own wish to live.

Ollie and Sally went for a walk in the early evening on Main Street. He had her hand in his. It guaranteed that she wouldn't do anything sudden, conspicuous, difficult, like walk into the street, like bang against a windowpane, like sit down all of a sudden and refuse to keep walking. But she didn't like to hold his hand. She liked to walk like everyone else. She had noticed that other women walked alone. She had asked for a pocketbook. He had bought one for her. It swung off her shoulder. He had put a wallet in it, with her name and home telephone number. He had put a lipstick and a compact in it too. She had been pleased.

Leah was waiting in line for the movie. She saw Ollie and Sally. Ollie stood next to her. Sally pulled at Leah's red sweater. Leah tried to move away. Sally hung on.

Leah said, "Red is my favorite color."

"Mine too," said Sally, "isn't it?" She turned to her brother. Her voice was deep, like a smoker's. Her eyelashes were long and dark; something graceful, elfin and innocent, flashed unexpected across her full face. Leah stared. Ollie took Sally's hand off Leah's sweater. The line moved forward. Ollie glided with it. Through the glass windows he watched Leah buy her ticket at the booth. Just before she

entered the theater she turned around and saw Ollie looking at her. That was good or maybe it wasn't.

Sally sat on her chair in the living room and plucked with
the fingers of her right hand at the seam of the arm. She
kicked with her feet at the floor. She was waiting for Ollie to
come home. It was Thursday and he had a faculty meeting
after school. He would be late. He had explained it to Sally.
He had shown her on the clock when he would arrive, the
little hand at six, the big hand at twelve. The big hand was
on the three and the little hand was past the six. Mrs.
Roomey was there. She cleaned. She looked after things.
She was Sally's friend. Mrs. Roomey was anxious to go
home. She was watching the clock too. She had her husband's dinner to fix. She had her purse in her hand. She had
her sweater on. Sally saw that it was almost dark. The tree
in the front lawn made a black shadow across the path. The
calico cat with the eye infection was sleeping outside on the
fallen leaves near the shed, near the wheels of the truck.
Sally went to the window and looked for the moon. She
didn't see it. She looked for the stars but it was too early.
The sky was only a pale gray. The streetlights went on. "You
wanna watch *Wheel of Fortune?*" said Mrs. Roomey. Sally
watched but while she watched she waited. She thought of
her mother. No more, she knew. She understood. Gone,
good-bye, flushed away, not here, never coming back. She
sat still. Emptiness was around her. Ollie, she thought,
waiting for the sound of his car coming down the block.
"Don't cry," she said to herself. She wiped her eyes with the
palms of her hands.

After the faculty meeting, which was unusually short because Hal Thomas, the principal, had barely survived root

canal work in the morning and was drowsy from painkillers and his jaw was swollen, Ollie drove over to Leah's house. He knew where it was. He had looked up the name in the book. It was listed under a Martin Rose. It was the only one it could be. The house was on a small street where his friends Laura and Peter Ellis lived. He had passed the house often but it had been dark, dark the way the summer people's houses usually were, spaces, silences, cold and moldy, waiting for light and voice to come into being, houses that were like rocks, inanimate. Ollie had learned as a child to ignore them, to pass them by as if they weren't there. As if they were under the sea, like submarines that only surfaced in the dark.

Now there was a light on. The car was in the driveway. There was a fire in the fireplace. She must have lit it herself. Ollie felt an aching in his arms. He would have lit it. He would have carried in the wood. He stopped his car across the street. What was he doing? He sighed. He felt naughty, as if he were a flasher about to jump from his car or a Peeping Tom who would wait till the darkness fell and then appear, eyes above the windowsill, to stare at the forbidden. He felt ashamed. He waited in his car. He watched the smoke come out the chimney. It was clear smoke, a good fire. He smiled. He knew something about her. She knew how to make a fire. He felt a weight in his body, a heaviness in his legs. He wanted. He wanted to see her in the window. He wanted to get out and peer in the window. He wanted her to come to the door. He willed her to come to the door. She didn't. He remembered her walking down the beach toward him. The back of his eyes hurt. He closed them. What was he doing? Waiting for what? Need made him notice the fading light, the loss of day. Finally he felt the dark grow deep around him. He was late. He started his car quickly, the rubber tires squeaked against the gravel of the road. Leah picked up her head from the book she was reading: *Moby Dick*.

Leah considered. When she had been a child in this house the adults had admired her: her father's friends. They had listened to her recite poems, watched her dance to the records her mother would play on the stereo. They had dunked bread in their coffee and blown smoke over her head. They had pinched her arms and hugged her waist. Her mother's friends had brought her presents, barrettes for her hair, a doll with a real cry, a box with a picture of a rose on the outside. The adults spoke to her in a halting English, a broken English or an English so elegant it had to be learned, new, polished each day. Among themselves they spoke German, or Yiddish, or something else. Among themselves they laughed at jokes she didn't understand, loud laughs that hit the ceiling and bounced back. They ate and ate till the dishes were piled so high in the sink that she worried they might break. They played cards. If she woke late at night and came downstairs they would be at the tables, and over the carpet everywhere were the crumbs of crackers and the shells of peanuts. The napkins would be crumpled and women's purses would be piled on the floor under the tables. The ashes would be spilling over from the glass ashtrays and the adults would be shouting at each other, roaring with sounds, their mouths open wide, rings on their fingers glistening in the light. Sometimes Leah would come down the stairs and they would be quiet, silently staring, each of them, off into a distance. There would be something else in the room, a waiting. Then her father would see her, he would shift in his chair and the babble would begin and the sound of clicking of the red nails of the women and the men rocking back on their chairs and the talk would grow and Leah would go upstairs, to bed, back to sleep, folding her dreams around her the way children do.

Sometimes Leah's mother baked prune dumplings and cookies in crescent shapes with vanilla bean and sugar coating. Leah came home from school and her mother was smiling in the doorway. What was learned? What was new? Leah's mother designed patterns for fabric, she designed clothes for a big manufacturer. She had a studio with paintbrushes, sketch pads, and bottles of water and colored ink. She had all Leah's clothes specially made. She had been a girl when she had left Vienna, in time, not her parents, not her brothers, just her, out in time. She had been brought to this country by a cousin and she had won a contest that gave her a job with a dress company and she had married the boss's nephew, who had also come in time, his gymnasium degree not yet in hand. He too was an orphan who was succeeding very well in his new home.

The house in West Pine had red-and-white-flowered cushions on the sofas and yellow walls and pictures of ships and whales and her mother's favorite, an Indian head in full dress with the great feathers hanging by his face. Indians, she said, are God's true children. Leah knew her mother didn't believe in God. Perhaps she didn't believe in Indians either.

Sometimes Leah came home from school to their city apartment on West End Avenue and her mother was in bed, sleeping. She was rumpled, still in her nightgown, and her eyes were dazed. There was a stale smell in her room, sweat and powder, perfume and steam heat. Leah's mother would move through the house picking up and putting down but never finishing anything. The iron was in the bathroom, the pots were on the floor. The curtains were lying across the chairs. The door to the studio was closed, the sketch pads unopened. Leah's mother did not play cards. She did not invite friends over. She was silent and when Leah asked her if she was sick, she would shake her head no. But Leah and her father had dinner at the corner Chinese restaurant night after night while her mother lay in her bed, floating in her thoughts, her wrists so thin that she could no longer wear her watch. This was how Leah learned that the mind is a mass of neurons and transmitters and that wires can fizzle and slip and that chemicals shift their balances and that even a mother can slide away, lock herself behind a door that can't be opened, not by a child who learns to brush her own hair and fix her own breakfast and comfort herself in the first moments of evening when the light gets odd and the distances between things grow. Leah learned how to lean against nothing, and still appear to be standing up straight.

Sometimes it was better. Her mother would go away for a while and come back smiling and kissing her and asking the names of her friends and offering to make her a dress of velvet. She would draw a picture and show Leah the dress that was to come. Sometimes it did, sometimes it didn't. Months of good times were followed by a return of the exhaustion, the closed doors, the averted face. Leah wasn't sure what began it, what ended it, when it would come. It wasn't her mother's fault. Her father had explained. She understood. It was no one's fault. Some minds were fragile, early losses, pain that no one else could see. Some minds could not stay the course. Leah would not be sad. Why should she? She had her own concerns. Everyone was amazed at Leah, who was so independent, so adult, so capable. No one had to worry about Leah.

One summer when things were going well, when they

were staying in West Pine and each Friday they would go to the train station, wait for the whistle, and Leah would run to her father, taking his briefcase in her arms and waving it in triumph to the skies, Leah's mother took her on a picnic to visit the Indian burial ground. There was nothing there but shrubs and cattails and sawgrass. There were thistles and clover and bushes. Out of their sight herds of deer loped, all innocence, brown eyes, white tails, past the brush, over the rose hips, the blackberries, the fallen twigs, the breeding mosquitoes, the high dune grass. Their hooves graced the long dead. Leah's mother had walked and walked. Leah waited near the car, where the picnic had been spread near the rear wheel in a clearing of sand. The mosquitoes were biting. The heat made her damp and her lips were dry. Butterflies, orange monarchs, dragonflies, drifted past.

"Let's go," said Leah.

"I'm thinking," said her mother. "Imagine," said her mother, "Indians were once here, camping in tents, fishing in the lake, paddling their canoes into the ocean, picking up clams and scallops in the bay. Their children making shell necklaces. The women stirring soup." Leah knew all that. "The Indians are gone, most all gone," said her mother. Leah watched her mother wiping her forehead with her arm. Leah packed up the picnic. Leah's mother rocked back and forth on her toes. "What are you doing?" said Leah. "Kaddish," said her mother. "It pays respect."

That was the summer that Leah's recurrent dream began. She was in an attic with a small window that looked out over a courtyard. In the attic there were boxes and boxes, old pipes and toilets ripped from their sites and lined like cemetery markers across the wooden floor. Leah was in the attic with her mother. Across the courtyard came the Nazis.

They were releasing pigeons from gold cages which were flying upward toward the attic. Leah and her mother took off their shoelaces and broke the neck of bird after bird as they entered through the open window. Leah's arms would grow tired. She leaned forward on the balls of her feet, focused her eyes as the pigeons came toward her. What if she missed the neck of the bird? Dead birds, with open beaks and twisted heads, were piled by her feet. Panic would rise like the tide in a heavy gale. Then she would wake in her bed. The dream continued all through the seasons and the years that followed.

Ollie had a dream. He woke up startled, his body in a sweat. His heart pounded. He wanted a woman. Whatever was in his dream it had made him groan and ache and desire. Briefly he had a high school sweetheart, Brenda Malcolm. Her parents did not approve. She let him kiss her. She let him touch over her brassiere. She once let him put his fingers under her skirt. He felt the tight cotton of her panties. Ollie lay in bed remembering his high school sweetheart while his body followed, panting heavily after his visions.

Now and then in the midst of a class, a teachers' meeting, while waiting in line at the IGA, while at the bank, he would see that he was alone, unnaturally alone. For a second, never more, he would pity himself. "You shithead," he would say to himself. "Shape up."

Sally walked out of the house into the backyard, where once the swing had been. It was a green metal set with a chain that connected the seat to the upper bar. She had swung in it a long time ago. Then her body got too big, her bottom wouldn't fit. The swing would tilt if she squeezed into it.

Her father took it down. One day it was gone, leaving brown spots on the grass where the poles had rested. Now there were two chairs, one for her, one for Ollie, chairs for lying in, the right size, made of plastic, red and blue. Sally lay down in her chair. The autumn sun was warm on her face. A line of geese crossed the blue sky above the trees on the side of the house. She could see their long necks extended forward. Birds, she said to herself. She stretched her arms up over her head. The muscles in her back relaxed. She reached her hand down into the wispy grass. She pulled at a dry blade. She brought it to her mouth. She ran her tongue over it. She smiled. The morning was new. The sun shadows were on the side of the house. Elijah jumped onto her lap. She rubbed his ears, sweet, she thought, sweet cat. He kneaded his paws into her jacket. He bumped his head into her chest, a ritual act, a cat habit. Sally lay still. She breathed softly, quietly, so the cat would stay with her. She wanted to twitch her arms, to flick her legs, but she didn't want the cat to startle. She made herself still. "Sweet," she said to the cat.

The cat saw something move behind the tree and left her. She let the blue sky stretch over her. She let herself float like she had as a child in the bathtub with her mother's hands holding her up. Good, everything was good. She tried to purr like the cat. The sound was funny. Good. In the flower beds, now cut back and covered with seaweed, Mrs. Roomey did it in September, Sally saw a winter daisy growing wild. She bent over and very carefully pulled it up.

She went into the house. She took off her jacket and put it on the hook. She went into the kitchen and handed the flower to Mrs. Roomey. "For me?" said Mrs. Roomey.

"Yes," said Sally. Sally went up to Mrs. Roomey. Sally was the larger and heavier and older of the two women. She

put her arms around Mrs. Roomey. She hugged her and in
the hug she crushed the daisy between them. Sally was
upset.

"It's fine," said Mrs. Roomey, who straightened out the
stem and unfolded the petals and put the flower in a glass.

"Good," said Sally when she saw the flower, not quite
standing, but leaning against the side of the glass, missing a
petal, but not bad, not close to dead, not yet.

Leah came out of her house on a Saturday morning planning to bicycle to town to buy her newspaper. She had a
three-speed, the one she used when her parents were alive,
the one they kept in the shed out back, and each spring it
was covered with cobwebs and rust. Each spring she would
polish it, put air in the tires, attach the basket that she kept
in the closet, and go ride, ride along the bluff and, guiding
the bike with her knees, put her hands in the air, till the
speed of the downhill made her dizzy, made the muscles in
her legs tremble, made her quit. Leah looked up as a neighbor's dog barked a deep lazy bark. Had he sighted a squirrel, a cloud, a wandering rabbit, a child chasing a ball or
something else, something more serious? Leah listened.
She saw Ollie Marcus in the road, outside her rhodo-
dendron bush, shifting uneasily, his eyes wide behind his
glasses, his arms hugging his broad chest, his slightly
bowed legs moving toward her.

What does he want? she thought. Was he dangerous?
Why did he make her nervous? What was he doing there, in
front of her house? Go away, she wanted to tell him. Whatever you're selling, I don't want it. No tickets to the firemen's
chicken barbecue, no opportunity to win a quilt, proceeds
for the sixth-grade trip to Washington, D.C. She didn't want
to sign a petition for a recall of a councilman. She didn't

want to contribute to the library cake sale. She didn't want to allow a zoning exemption for the fitness club. She didn't care if developers took the Indian burial ground. She just wanted to be left alone. Or did she?

It was into that slight opening that Ollie stepped. "I just came to see if you needed anything."

"What would I need?" she answered.

"Do you need more wood? It's going to get cold," he said.

"I know," she said. "I plan ahead." She pushed her bike forward.

He followed. "Are you writing a book? People come here to write books."

"No," said Leah. "I'm a research scientist. I'm here to think. I need peace and quiet," she added, scowling at him slightly.

"Quiet is its own kind of noise," he said, feeling foolish; that was like a Zen phrase, one hand clapping, one foot without a sock, a universe that vibrates but doesn't mean. An affectation, a desperate bid for attention. He flinched. She saw it.

"That's true," she said. Although she wasn't sure what was true. Instead she said, "How's Sally?" Then she wanted to say, What's wrong with Sally, Has she always been like that? But she knew it was cruel to speak of handicaps. It was cruel even to observe them. Keep your eyes away from the stumps of beggars. Keep your eyes away from the burn marks on faces. Ignore the smallness of dwarfs and the canes of the blind. Pretend everything is normal. She had no more words.

"Sally is with Mrs. Roomey. She helps me out," he said. "I was wondering if you would walk with me this morning along the beach." The worst that could happen is she would say no. Who cares, he thought.

"Oh," said Leah. A walk on the beach, a man and woman walking on the beach, what was so wrong with that?

So no became yes and yes became now and the bike was put back in the shed and Leah was surprised at herself. She should have said no. It would have been better, safer. Who knew about this man? He could be mad. He could be a rapist. He could be a con man after her funds. They had not been introduced by a mutual friend. She thought it was all right to go for a walk, but don't under any circumstances, she reminded herself, let him into the house.

On the walk Ollie told Leah about his honors seminar, none of them had passed out in class yet, one football player with an elbow smashed during the tryouts. He told her about his collection of Hemingway first editions. He told her how as a young man he had wanted to go to Vietnam and save the country, but the time had passed. The moment was over. Each generation had its own story. Or lack of it, he added. He had been needed at home. He had gone to the East Pine branch of the state college. He had deferments. He shrugged. His lips parted in a smile.

"You might have been killed," said Leah.

"I would have seen the Orient. I might have become a dealer in jade or bamboo," said Ollie.

"Would that have been better?" asked Leah.

"Who knows," said Ollie.

He liked talking to Leah. They sat down on a rotted piece of driftwood and Ollie stared out at the water. Leah stared after him. He also liked not talking to Leah. Up the beach, by the dunes where the wooden stakes placed by the park service held in the sand against winter storms, a boy and his father were flying a kite, a red kite with a long orange tail. It caught in the wind and soared and the boy ran with it. "Watch out," yelled the father, "watch out for the fence, look where you're going." The boy ran on.

Ollie stole a look at Leah's face turned toward the sea where the light on the whitecaps came down from the sky streaked, cloud-stained, scattered. His hands, stuffed in his pockets, moved. He had a thought that he immediately censured. He wanted to save this woman from danger. What danger? What nonsense? What sexism sat in his belly. He loathed himself while with even more ferocity the thought rose again. Watch over her, it said, and with that his body swelled with longing and he dug his heels deep into the sand. Was he the source of the danger?

Leah picked up a horseshoe crab shell. It was almost whole. She turned it over and, holding it by its thin hard tail, examined the small dried-up legs and the sand-filled spine. "A billion years on the planet," said Leah.

"Long time," said Ollie.

"I'm interested in fossils," said Leah.

"Good," said Ollie. "I think I am one."

"Not yet," said Leah, who hadn't been trained in metaphor. Ollie turned his face away toward the horizon.

"I've been imagining," he said, "why you are here without a mate. I have several ideas, do you want to hear them?"

"Yes," said Leah, who did but was also embarrassed. There was shame to her aloneness, a public failure, as if she were a dwarf or a three-breasted woman, a member of a traveling freak show.

Ollie counted, "One: leprosy picked up on a tropical island when you were researching a rare one-celled animal.

Two: love for a married scientist at your lab. Three: you were attached to a man who preferred men . . ."

"Sorry," Leah interrupted, "it's nothing like that."

"What?" said Ollie.

Leah said, "I work. I care about my work. I think about it all the time." Ollie was quiet. "Also," she said, "old maids live longer. Did you know that?"

"No," said Ollie, "but I believe it." He waited.

"I'm used," she said, "to being alone."

"Let's walk," he said and turned partly away from her. She would be frightened. He knew she would be frightened if she saw his desire and knew she was its object.

But Leah was calm. It was natural to walk on the beach with this man who was talking now about a student of his, a boy who had rescued his two younger brothers from a fire. He was talking about instant bravery. The kid was brave. Ollie talked on and on and needed little response. He was telling her about a girl whose mother was ill and how she came to school late and half-asleep. "Not fair," he said. Leah listened. This was a man who still hoped that things would be fair. Ha, thought Leah. He moved near her, his wide body stepping over piles of seaweed, his boots leaving prints in the sand, between the tire marks of a jeep that had recently been through. They sat down on the sand. His suggestion. She looked at the sea, not thinking anything at all, letting it rise and fall, hit the shore and recede, as if she were a pebble left there to age in dignity, in peace. Later as they were walking back toward her house she looked at him quickly. His curly hair was blowing upward in irregular tufts. His glasses were misted over, the air was damp, the sea was close. He kept taking off his glasses and wiping them on his sleeve. They weren't young. She knew that neither of them was young, which was why there was so much weight in their steps. It was too much. She didn't invite him in for coffee. It might be dangerous to let him in her house, a man who complained at the unfairness of things. She waved good-bye to him from the yard.

She took her bicycle and went to town for the paper. She put him out of her head. That evening she thought of him like the kite they had seen, a dazzling color in someone else's hand dipping up and down, impressions on her retina, sent back to the brain, organized, interpreted, pupil contracting, optic nerve racing, a kite had sailed by her eye and then was gone.

Myrna called. "My gold pin, the one I think she stole. I think she stole it and used the money for a stash."

"How do you know?" said Leah.

"Red eyes, snuffling, averting her head, droopy behavior, silences. That's how," Myrna said.

"What are you going to do?" asked Leah.

"Save her," said Myrna.

"How?" said Leah.

"Find her stash and feed it to the snake," said Myrna.

"Christ," said Leah.

"Don't marry a man with a child," said Myrna. "In fact, don't marry a man. Find a nice German shepherd with a good thick coat."

"I met a man who lives with his peculiar sister," said Leah.

"How peculiar."

"Very."

"Avoid him," said Myrna.

"I will," said Leah.

*   *   *

Ollie was shaving. He cut himself. A deep cut. The blood ran down the basin. He watched the blood. "Fuckup," he said to himself. Then he felt sick.

Sally sat by the television eating chicken that had been fried by Mrs. Roomey in the morning. She was wearing a big pair of slacks and a blue and white T-shirt that said "West Pine 43." Ollie had found it under a bench in the boys' locker room. Howard Forrest had left it behind when he was suddenly sent to juvenile detention at Hillsdale for breaking into a summer house, stealing a stereo, making himself a steak from the freezer, and leaving greasy fingerprints as well as melting ice cream all over the living room couch. Howard Forrest had been the tight end for the team and so his jersey was just the right size for Sally. Ollie had visited Howard Forrest every week. He spoke to the parole officer. He spoke to the social worker. He helped arrange for an uncle in Massachusetts to take the boy when his term was over. He got a Christmas card last year from Howard that didn't say how he was doing, which is what Ollie wanted to know. Instead under the little lambs and the shining star it said, in barely legible script, "Bart Simpson for President."

She loves her television, said Mrs. Roomey to Ollie. He knew it. She watched the commercials and tears came to her eyes when puppies appeared, when fathers reached out to pat their sons on the shoulder, when mothers touched the newly washed dresses of their daughters. She gasped with pleasure when birthday cakes were served. She laughed when people slipped and fell, when animals talked, when cartoon characters chuckled. She smiled at rainbows and stars twinkling and the gleam on glasses taken from the dishwasher. The set was always on. Even if Sally was eating in the kitchen or had gone upstairs to her room, the set was on. If Ollie turned it off before she was deeply asleep, she would call out to him. He thought of it as her umbilical cord, attaching her to the world outside, keeping her, by way of satellite dish, by way of cable tower, connected to the others. She watched tennis matches and *Star Trek*. At night sometimes Ollie would come downstairs and see the blue light of the tube flickering in the living room. Sally would be there watching old movies. She didn't need much sleep. She liked the old movies. "See how funny they walk," she said. "See how they smoke. See how they drink." "Go to bed, it's late," Ollie would say. Sally would smile at him. "A little bit longer. A little bit." He would go back to bed. In the morning he often found her asleep in the armchair that had been his father's favorite, her head back, her tongue making those familiar darts in and out, and her breathing heavy and steady. He would turn off the television so that he could read his paper in quiet.

The only time he wanted to watch television was Monday nights and Sunday afternoons when football was on. Especially he loved the Giants. Sally watched with him. She cheered when he cheered. She glowered when he glowered. "Goddamn bastard," Ollie would call out. "Blockhead," he would scream. Sally would scream with him, "Run, turn around, not so far, stop him, fucking asshole, asshole." It was the replays that got him. The ball had been dropped. They showed it again, the player had his arms raised, his left foot up in the air. "This time do it right," Ollie would mutter. He would stare as the quarterback released the ball and it floated up toward the tight end, knowing better, knowing it had already happened, hoping for an alteration, a break in the time loop, a chance to do it again. He stared riveted as they showed the same play in slow motion, then again from another angle. His body was frozen, he didn't breathe.

Sally liked the halftime shows. He watched them with her. She waved back at the cheerleaders, boom, boom, boom, she pretended her thighs were a drum. When his team lost, he felt battered. He was mean and hurt. When they won, contentment flooded his bones and the blood stopped boiling in his veins. Often he took a nap.

After his mother had died he braided Sally's hair in front of the television. She was less apt to complain if the comb caught a snag. He would bend her head forward while she sat on the floor and he sat cross-legged on the blue armchair behind her. First he brushed one hundred times, to keep the shine, the way his mother had done. Then carefully he would begin the plaits, first one side and then the other. Sally would toss her head impatiently if he didn't also touch her shoulder from time to time, if he didn't also talk to her right over the sound of the television. It was in those moments before he had gotten the rubber bands across the bottom of the braids that he would tell her about his students, who had said what, who was friends with whom, who was sad, who was getting fat, who was always boasting, who was dreaming out the window, what was happening with his fellow teachers, who had gotten married, who had moved away, who was fighting with whom on the faculty. Just as his mother had accompanied the braiding of Sally's hair with the stories of the store, who had come, who had bought, who had paid, who had charged, what she knew and what she wondered, and what might be one day, how the weather had changed, what the price of a new dress might be, so he chanted his observations to Sally while he braided her hair and she would sit quietly until he was through.

Years before Sally had asked him to buy her a Barbie doll. For several years she took it with her up and down the stairs, into the bathroom, out on their walks, into town, a large woman, limping, holding in her good hand a Barbie doll. For years it sat on the table next to her when she had dinner. She kissed it. She stuffed it into her shirt, and so the wavy blond head and the startled blue eyes would appear like a strange homunculus, like the angel with a message in a medieval painting riding the beam into the Virgin's ear. Sally kept Barbie tucked under her pillow when she went to sleep. Barbie lost an arm. Barbie's hair fell out. Ollie bought a replacement. Ollie bought all the clothes, the party dress, the alpine hiking shorts, the stewardess uniform complete with overnight bag, the tennis shorts, the bathing suit. Sally had trouble changing the outfits. Sometimes Ollie would do it for her, his broad fingers struggling with tiny pearl buttons, with little lamé jackets, with leather skirts.

Once Sally said to him, "Why not me?" He wanted not to understand. He ignored her. She asked again. He sat down on the floor with her. Her heavy thighs bounced up and down.

"Mama told you," he said.

"Tell me again," she said.

"You're different," he said. "It can't be helped. It can't be changed. You have your own way, your own Sally ways, you're special. Not like others, but good too. Very good." He said, "Forget it."

Sally looked at him. She bit at her thumb. "Not good," she said. "Not good. Not good like everyone, like Barbie." Ollie remembered the way her eyes looked, the way her mouth turned, the way the tongue sat when she finished saying it.

Sally took the Barbie doll and hid it under the couch. Dust balls gathered and stuck on Barbie's face. Ollie retrieved it. Sally hid it again. It never reappeared. To know what has been lost is worse than losing it. Ollie did not know how to make Sally ignorant.

Sally was watching TV, her supper on a tray on her lap. Ollie was at the table. The tomato sauce on his spaghetti was cooling and congealing. He was reading instead of eating. He couldn't concentrate. He read the same paragraph over and over. He stood up and stretched his legs. Elijah rubbed at his knees. The house was a blaze of lights, as if someone were trying to banish the shadows. He thought of the bill. Damn — he didn't have the money to keep the dark at bay all through the night, in every corner of his house. He went into his parents' bedroom. Sally had put the lights on there. He breathed in the mildew that came from the still air. He opened a window. He turned out the lights and closed the door. He flicked off the hall light, the bathroom light, and the bare bulb in the attic that was attached by an old chain. The chain came off in his hand, he pulled so hard.

"I want the lights on," said Sally.

"I don't," said Ollie.

"Light," Sally shouted at him.

"I want to put them out for a while," said Ollie in his most reasonable voice. "Finish your dinner," he said.

"Finish yours," said Sally.

He thought for a moment. Was it worth it, the battle that was building? He retraced his steps. He turned on the lights, one by one. He left the door to his parents' bedroom open so Sally could see the light if she looked up. Damn the bill, he thought, unable to stop thinking of it until he thought of Leah Rose.

Why did she seem so aloof? Did she have a secret? Had she been burned across her body in a childhood accident? Had she lost a breast? Was she frigid and afraid of men? Was she one of those women who bore a grudge, who heard voices, who had been jilted or ignored at some crucial moment after which nothing would matter? Naturally she hadn't been able to tell him. Would she? Her face at least was untouched. He knew it was fine, fine enough to come again and again into his mind, surprising him, startling him into a new awakeness, a mild electric shock, a sudden leap of concentrated joy.

Sally was watching cartoons. The turtles were fighting and there was a spaceship and the stars had eyes and were looking down at the children turtles. There were crackles and explosions. Sally put her hands up over her ears. Loud noises made her worry. Worry that something was breaking. That she had done something that she shouldn't, that something was wrong. The space rockets and the laser guns on the television splayed light across the screen. Then there were three children eating Jell-O and smiling. Sally smiled back at them. "Good," she said.

Ollie came in the room, Sally came over and sat on the floor near him. When she sat down there was a plop as her heavy legs hit the floor. She looked startled. "Don't worry, sweetpuss," said Ollie. His hand was on her shoulder. She put her head against his leg and rested there. He touched her hair. She leaned her body against his thigh. She petted his shoe. Her face was calm and her eyes were clear. Despite the heaviness in her features he saw that she looked like Debra Winger, older, of course, thicker, but something in the shape of the mouth, in the slope of the nose, something in the coloring, the pale skin, the dark hair, something open and illuminated, as if the shine came from within, a bright bulb swinging round, like a lighthouse. Ollie squeezed her neck gently. "Good," she said.

*　　*　　*

Leah saw Dr. André Sonnabend, a man in his sixties, nearly bald, with a gray mustache and a thin pale face, in the parking lot in front of the IGA. Aren't you the Roses' daughter? he said. "I am," said Leah. He introduced himself, and his wife, Litzie, a small-boned older woman, slight and tiny, with her hair cropped close to her skull, and large eyes that invited Leah to come nearer. "Do you remember me?" he said. Leah did. The first summer her mother had locked herself in her room, when her father had sat in the kitchen with his glass of tea, stirring and stirring it, Dr. Sonnabend, a vacationing psychiatrist, one of her parents' friends, had sat down in the kitchen with her father. She had waited in the hall. She listened to the rise and fall of their words. She remembered how heavy her legs had seemed. A spider in the corner dropped a line from her web and hung suspended in the still August air. Her father had stood up and made a decision. Leah remembered Dr. Sonnabend sitting cross-legged on the floor outside her parents' bedroom. Her father leaning against the wall. Dr. Sonnabend talking, muttering, soothing tones, promises, some German, some English, till her mother, with dark circles under her eyes, with a stained nightgown, opened the door to him and he entered and the door closed. Later her father drove her mother off to the hospital. Her father's cousin had arrived on the train and stayed with Leah.

Now in the parking lot of the IGA the Sonnabends seemed glad to see her. They were part of her childhood. "We're here on weekends. You must come see us," Litzie Sonnabend said. In West Pine there were people who still remembered her parents. The dead lived on in the minds of the living, like the smoke from an extinguished candle, the soul left a trace for a brief second, in minds of kith and kin.

*   *   *

Leah called her friend Myrna. "What's it like, with only lo-cals around?" asked Myrna.

"All right," said Leah. "I'm doing all right. I met some old friends of my parents. Psychoanalysts. They're here on weekends. They told me to stop by."

"That's all?" said Myrna.

"Essentially," said Leah.

"But who do you talk to?" asked Myrna.

"You," said Leah.

"What about time, doesn't it hang, doesn't it slop over you or something? Do you get dressed, do you take care of yourself? People can lose their minds if they go to a cabin by the sea and think, just think." Leah sighed. "Well, is any-thing happening to you?" said Myrna.

Leah paused. "Something is happening to me."

"What?" said her friend.

"I don't know yet," said Leah. "When I know I'll tell you."

"My stepdaughter is considering Scientology," said Myrna. "She jumps when I enter the room. My pearls that my mother gave me when I graduated from high school are missing. They had a ruby clasp. Do you think she took them? My dentist told me he's a codependent. My mother is taking Prozac. I'm illustrating a book for children four to eight that discusses anxiety in the age of divorce. My super is on vacation and there is a brown stain in the tub. Some-thing in the pipes. Something smells terrible in our bath-room. I've cleaned and cleaned. It still smells. Something is rotting in our bathroom. You're the scientist, Leah. What's in my bathroom?"

Leah said, "It's either bacteria from a feces backup in the plumbing or it's your imagination."

"The snake," said Myrna, "it doesn't seem to be eating,

the last mouse was only half-consumed. Do snakes get sick?"

"I don't know," said Leah, who was succumbing to exhaustion.

"What about the man with the repulsive sister?" said Myrna.

"I don't know," said Leah.

"Push him away," said Myrna. "God forbid you should have a sexual encounter, a romance, a love affair, a touching of souls."

"I don't need sarcasm," said Leah.

"I just hate to see you drying up. Time is short, you know," said Myrna.

"I've done all right," said Leah. "At least I have all my jewelry."

Leah walked into her parents' room. Her mother's clothes, some of her own designs, were still in her closet. Leah had once packed them all to take back to the city, to give to a homeless shelter. But then she had unpacked them and hung everything back in the closet. Her father's red flannel shirt, his khaki pants, his hip-high rubber boots for clamming, were all there. The room was dark. On the dresser was a photograph of Leah building a sand castle. Her long hair flying in the air, unbrushed. In the dresser were her father's passport and her mother's too, under the letters Leah had written from Paris, where she had gone to work in a lab the summer after she graduated from college. The letters were tied together with a purple ribbon. Leah touched them but did not open the packet. She left her parents' bedroom. Perhaps she should leave. Go back to work. Take a trip to Italy. Go to the conference on cellular electricity being held in Bonn. Drifting, she was drifting. She was deliberately not thinking about Ollie Marcus and his huge sister.

Offshore, the large blues, some over fourteen pounds, their silver scales heaving as they circled in the dark waters, moved deep under. The cold was coming. The jellyfish, large, with purple tentacles stretching downward toward the mud and coral, the rock and weed of the distant bottom, floated, thousands of them, brought with the tides from the other side of the world. The icy eye of the navy lighthouse flashed across the waters, beaming light where darkness belonged. All through the night, Ollie tossed on his bed. He thought of Leah Rose and her hair tumbling out of its barrette. He thought of Leah Rose slipping out of her skirt and turning toward him. He thought of Leah Rose reaching her hand forward and touching his face, running her fingers down over his lips. He thought about calling her at two in the morning. Perhaps she was up. He stopped himself. She was asleep. She was not thinking of him. She was riding through her own night sky. He felt space around his bed, a wide swath of dead space. He heard the TV humming from downstairs. He turned on the light and was not comforted.

In the morning in the kitchen, fixing breakfast for Sally, scrambled eggs and juice, he took a glass from the cupboard and dropped it on the floor. He opened his fingers and let it fall. Then he had to sweep up the pieces. Mop with the wet mop and run a towel across the floor into all the cracks of the tile. Often Sally forgot to wear shoes and roamed the house barefoot.

Ben Morris, who taught math, the old gym teacher who did pelvic tilts on the locker room floor, Nancy Harris, who was assistant to the principal and whose dentist husband had drilled and dug in Ollie's gums, they had long since

stopped fixing him up. He would come to dinner. He would
be polite. He would take the woman home. He took a few
women out, to dinner at Mackie's on the highway, to a picnic
in the state park, to the Elks Club fair over in East Pine. The
women, women who were patient, eager, hopeful, with
shiny hair and eyes that understood, gentle women, brisk
women, sexy women, tennis players, social workers, a reading disability teacher, a woman who ran her father's plumbing firm, a town clerk, an emergency room nurse, pure
women, innocent women, recovering women, women so
young they had no stories to tell, women nearer his age
who knew better than to tell their stories, women who
couldn't have children, women who wanted children,
women with children who had to get baby-sitters for the
night, all these he had come near and then pulled away
from. Not for him, not now, not ready, not possible, no
chemistry, no wish, no time, no. He knew they had urgent
needs. He moved back from the sharp smell of expectation
that moved with them across each room. He knew he
would disappoint them. He knew he couldn't do it, not all
the way, not joint checking accounts, not sharing tooth-
brushes, not repairing old holes in the garment of self.
Sometimes he spent the night. He released his body onto
theirs. He lay down in their beds. He felt warmth, gratitude, even admiration. He had to leave. When the high
school drama club did a performance of *Fiddler on the Roof,*
Kevin Howe the drama teacher told Ben Morris that he
thought Ollie needed a professional matchmaker. "Too
bad," said Kevin, "there are none in West Pine." Mrs.
Roomey told her husband, who worked for Eastern Electric,
that Ollie Marcus was too busy reading to get married.
"That man has his head in a book all the time. A waste,"
she said, " 'cause he has potential."

Ben Morris brought up the theory of latent homosexuality to the principal, who believed it. But Ollie Marcus didn't appear at restaurants with the decorators, the antique collectors, the restorers. He had appeared at the fund-raiser for the AIDS quilt but so had every religious leader in town and all the businessmen and the principal himself. Besides, Ollie was one of those teachers who hold a school together, a kind of invisible pillar that keeps the sides up. The new teachers asked him for help, the old ones pushed to sit at his table in the lunchroom. The kids lied as easily as they breathed but they told Ollie Marcus the truth at least some of the time. As long as he doesn't touch any of our boys, it's none of my business, the principal decided, a man's private life is his own. And of course Ollie Marcus has to take care of his sister. In his own way he's a family man.

Ollie considered lechery, bawdiness, lewdness. He thought of biological need. The testosterone levels rising, the pulse racing, the puffing of sperm sac. Ollie considered that Leah Rose had captured his heart and his heart was in his body and his body was prey to vulgar thoughts and the heat of the moment. Of course it was all right. Why shouldn't he have unclean thoughts? He wasn't married. He didn't want to get married. This was a mere adventure. He could permit himself an adventure. One every fifteen years, he said to himself, will keep the rust from my limbs. He would never let it get out of control, take more than its apportioned time or stray from its leashed place. He was in no danger of losing control. He was a man disciplined and cautious, used to his ways. There was no risk in pursuing a woman who was visiting, who was staying just a while, who had shown no particular interest in him, who seemed to want nothing that he might offer, a woman so educated that she had a doctorate while he had only his master's from the teachers college in the next county. He had never left home. She was experienced, traveled to conferences around the world, knew scientists from Vienna and Paris. She had told him that. So he was a bumpkin with a game to play. If he lost he lost. It wouldn't matter. He had nothing to worry about. He worried anyway but that was his habit.

The next afternoon he appeared at Leah's door. The day had been brilliant clear but now the light was fading, as if the sun were holding its breath, averting its face, bending its head away from the globe. There were pale orange patches over the window lintels, over the roof. She opened the door and looked at him. What did he want? Why was he there? She was confused. Was she supposed to say something? Was there something she should have done? Behind him the last of the bees were flying from one dried bud to another. In the yard her hose lay neatly folded like a large snake digesting.

"Leah," he said, "thought you might like these." In one hand he held a miniature tree of broccoli, its deep green stem circled with a cord, its buds tight together, dark violet. In the other hand he held a butternut squash, bell-shaped, deep yellow, its orange seeds set in a moist thready center, waiting for a signal to heat and split. He had passed the roadside wagon on his way back from the girls' field hockey game at Brighton. West Pine had triumphed but Mandy Session, center forward on the Lady Whalers team, had lost a front tooth when the opposing right back had raised her stick beyond the permissible height. Blood had poured. Ollie responded with an increased heartbeat as if he had been running up and down the field instead of sitting in the stands. He had felt faint but steadied himself. It was embarrassing to be so affected. So the comforting sight of broccoli and squash had soothed his agitation. His pulse had slowed.

Leah saw him there, his jacket open, his curly hair un-
kempt, his ears sticking out, pink from the cool wind. His
glasses held tight to the bridge of his nose. Leah took the
broccoli and the squash. Behind her on the TV the weather
girl was standing before the satellite pictures of clouds covering the northeast, the clouds moved eastward. The camera
rewound and the clouds jerked back a few inches.

"It's going to rain," said Leah.

"I know," said Ollie. "I heard it on the news."

"Would you like some coffee?" said Leah. Her voice was
thin, proper, strained. Coffee was what her parents always
offered their guests.

"Yes," said Ollie, who didn't want coffee but wanted to
say yes.

In the kitchen, Leah filled the pot with water, arranged
the filter, took out two cups. Ollie watched her back stretching up and leaning down.

Leah said, "I don't like the parts in *Moby Dick* about
whaling and tools and ropes. It goes on too long."

Ollie said, "Patience, people have lost their patience."

Leah said, "Why should I care about the length of har-
poons?"

Ollie said, "You need to believe, to know that the writer
knows, that the sea is not a fiction and the men on it are
engaged in work, life-and-death work. You need the details
to know, to really know that place, that event, the whale
may be a symbol, may be a madman's vision, but he's still a
whale, turning over, sinking down, rising to the top of a
real sea."

"Oh," said Leah.

Ollie said, "Are you afraid of me?"

Leah said, "No."

Ollie said, "Why are you sitting all the way across the room?" Leah moved closer.

Ollie said, "I have no friends who are summer people."

Leah said, "So?"

"So," said Ollie, "I've never been here in this house before."

"You came," said Leah.

"I know," said Ollie.

"You can leave if you want," said Leah.

"No," said Ollie, "not yet. I haven't finished my coffee."

Leah said, "Were you married?"

"No," said Ollie.

"Why not?" said Leah.

"I have Sally," said Ollie. "Besides, I am an odd man, maybe too odd."

"What's odd about you?" said Leah. "What do you mean 'odd'?"

"Nothing," said Ollie.

There was silence. "I'm odd too," said Leah.

"How?" said Ollie.

"I just am," said Leah. Ollie leaned forward and put his hand on Leah's. She did not jump or pull her hand away.

Ollie said, "I wish I had known you when you were a girl."

Leah said, "Why?"

Ollie said, "Then I would understand you."

Leah said, "No you wouldn't." Ollie put his fingers around her hand.

"You've given up hope," he said.

"No," said Leah. A single tear, unwanted, unexpected, appeared in her left eye. It was followed by another one. "My parents died," she said in explanation.

"Everyone's parents die," said Ollie.

"Yes," said Leah. Ollie leaned forward and put his arms around Leah. She did not pull away.

"I don't know you," said Leah.

"I have no diseases," said Ollie.

"I don't know you," said Leah again.

"You will," said Ollie, who believed it.

"I don't have any diseases either," said Leah.

Leah sighed, Ollie sighed. They both knew that their private story couldn't be easily summed up, presented like a passport at the border of a new country. They both knew that what had happened before was better saved for another time.

"I really am a patient woman," said Leah.

"Good," said Ollie. He reached over and touched her neck just below her ear with his forefinger. He drew a line from her ear to her collarbone and left his finger there. She shivered. The TV repeated the temperatures for the next day in the tri-state area and reported that high tide would come at 4:03 in the morning. Ollie slid his fingers down the top of her blouse. She put her hands on his knees and searched his face. She was looking for cruelty, indifference, hardness, dullness. She found only the slightly wrinkled, crumpled look of a man in want. Leah said, "Your mother should have taped your ears down to your head when you were a baby. Then they would lie flat now." Ollie put his hand further down her blouse. She was surprised. She had never known before that a pulsing in her nipple could run right down into the base of her spine. "Oh," she said. "I don't do this all the time," she added.

"Neither do I," he said, getting up to turn off the TV. Ollie put his head in Leah's lap. He looked up at her. Her black hair hung like a curtain over her brains. The weight of his head pressed into her. She felt a curling within, a pulling tight of invisible cords, a heaviness as if she had swallowed a rock, a burning of the labia, a smoldering, a calling out of tissue to tissue, flesh to flesh, a pleading of body against the reasons of the mind, a desire to fall forward into the ooze of dividing amoebas, into the mud where self became species, a puffing of fluids, a dancing of nerve endings, nothing mysterious, all biological. She rocked back and forth on her hips, staring down into the face of Ollie Marcus.

How was she odd? he wondered. Did she wash the dishes over and over again? Did she keep old newspapers? Did she get frightened in crowds? Did she practice animal sacrifice? Did she think men were apes or rapists?

What was wrong with him? she considered. Could he be gay trying to switch because of health fears? Could he be a womanizer, the kind who conquered compulsively and bragged about it later? Could he be a man with irregular desires? Would he ask her to spank him or dress him in her underwear? No handcuffs, she would never let a man slip handcuffs on her. She glared at Ollie.

On her bed, on her single child's bed, she lay down, still and waiting. He leaned over and unbuttoned her blouse. He lifted her breasts one by one out of their binders. He reached a hand behind and undid the clasp. Slowly, as if time were stopped, as if everyone weren't mortal and the future uncertain, he pulled at her jeans till they slid off her legs. She moved not at all. She helped him in no way. She was frozen, inert, still. She lay on the bed naked. His fingers trailing up and down. Her long body was marked with the scar of her appendectomy. Also there was a red raised jagged line on her forearm from a chemical burn in the lab. Her breasts hung low, her thighs were broad, her navel was stretched wide. Her neck was already showing signs of release, of gatherings, of folds under the chin. He slipped his hands over her hips, wide and full. He noticed the stretch marks, the mole on her collarbone, the freckles on her hips. He pressed his palms down over her torso. She rocked gently on the bed. He was standing over her naked. His back was not altogether straight, one leg was a little longer than the other. The hairs of his chest were black and gray and curly. His eyes without the glasses stared and struggled for focus. "Is it raining yet?" she said. "A cold front is moving in." He put his fingers over her mouth. He leaned his body over hers. He stayed there waiting till she grew accustomed to him.

The rain began on the roof, he could hear it beating softly on the pane. The doll's house in the corner creaked as the bed moved on the wooden floor.

Afterward he lay there motionless. They were cramped on the bed. She felt cold on her spine. Then she pulled the daisy-patterned comforter over them both and closed her eyes and fell toward sleep. Darkness. Leah turned on the light. His lips had settled in something like a smile. Sweetness. His face had forgotten what it knew. He sat up. He remembered. He looked at his watch. "I have to go home."

"Of course," said Leah.

The Methodist Church was holding a bake sale to benefit its roof-repair project. The Animal Rescue Fund was having its annual art auction at the Lions Club. The combined junior high schools of East and West Pine were giving a performance of *Grease*. The pumpkins were huge in the fields and the city people could stop and pick their own on their way back to town. The leaves were almost all down. Every house had a pile in the front and a pile in the back, and the town carters moved up and down the streets collecting the leaves that the wind didn't blow away, smashing the twigs that gathered in the muddy gutters. The dune grass was pale and bent low and the sand blew about in small cloudbursts above the high-water mark. The lifeguard stands were pulled up into the shack on the dunes. The orange rubber rescue raft was jammed behind the locked door. The electric-blue trash bins that in full season received Popsicle wrappers, soda cans, diapers, tangled fishing line, broken kites, and empty bottles of suntan lotion had been removed to the town garage, where they were stored in groups of three. A king crab crawled along the shore, blindly moving toward a pile of broken shells. The cold water heaved and swelled, the horizon met the sky where the earth sloped away. The ocean sounded its call, slap, wash, and a hoarse clearing of throat, sloshing and banging, growling again and again. The autumn wind swept the beach smooth. Leah Rose walked, swinging her arms in her jacket. The weather would hold for another two days. She breathed deeply. Salt settled in her hair and her lungs.

She had called her friend Myrna. "My bathroom still stinks," said Myrna. "I've called a plumber. I called an emergency number, but he won't come until next week."

Leah said, "I have a new friend."

"A male friend?" asked Myrna.

"Yes," said Leah.

"The one with the peculiar sister?" said Myrna.

"Yes," said Leah.

"Couldn't you find someone free?" said Myrna.

"Couldn't you?" said Leah.

"How many years has it been?" said Myrna.

"A while," said Leah.

"Tell me," said Myrna.

"Not yet," said Leah. "There's nothing to tell you yet. I may never see him again."

"So why did you tell me in the first place?" said Myrna.

"I want you to know I'm still alive out here."

"Wonderful," said Myrna.

"I'm not a romantic moon-spoon type."

"No," said Myrna, "you're not."

"But I've had an experience."

"My stepdaughter told me I have crossed eyes. My eyes are not crossed," said Myrna. "I wore a patch when I was a child. They were fixed. My gold watch is gone."

"I'm sorry," said Leah.

"The superintendent says the building put in new plumbing three years ago. Nothing could be wrong. But the bathroom stinks. It really stinks," said Myrna.

"Get a second opinion," said Leah.

"I think of you," said Myrna.

"Don't ever stop," said Leah.

After school Ollie went to Leah's house. She was in the back, in the garden, cutting things down, covering the earth with seaweed. She was wearing heavy gloves, dark pants, and a hat to keep her ears warm. The wind came off the sea. Leah saw Ollie. "Sometimes my mother would do this," she said. Ollie nodded. He always felt awkward in gardens. His mother hadn't planted, pruned, sheared, or weeded. She thought the ladies with their petunias and their lilies were wasting their time. "Hoity-toity," she said.

"Leah," he said. "I'm teaching tonight at the Senior Citizens' Center. I'm teaching Walt Whitman. You could come. Talk to them. You could talk about the cell. The class would be pleased to hear from a real scientist. Afterward we could have coffee." His mind was numb. His mouth said the words. He had rehearsed them. He braced himself for disappointment. She might have considered him a one-night stand. Women now took men that way. Just for the borrowing, the pleasure that came and went. Only a small muscle twitch in the back of his thigh told him that he was waiting.

Leah was silent. She looked at Ollie. He was wearing a jacket, a tie, his school clothes. He took a step backward. She wanted to say no. She liked being alone. After dinner she had planned to stretch out on her bed and draw. Draw pictures of bacteria. She thought something might come if she drew them again, the way she had as a student. She had things to do. She didn't need him to ask her to the Senior Citizens' Center and out for coffee. He wanted a free lecture. Had the senior citizens asked him to recruit her? "How lucky we are, ladies and gentlemen, to have an expert spending the winter right here in West Pine." She wanted to say no but she didn't. She said, "What time?"

He said, "Seven. Sally is coming. She has friends at the center." He turned to go.

Leah wanted to call after him, I just remembered I can't. I'm engaged tonight. I don't really feel well. Maybe some other time. She wanted to call after him but she didn't. She didn't want to go anywhere with his sister.

Ollie had the old folks pull their chairs in a circle around him. He first read several pages of *Song of Myself*. Then he asked them about immortality, what did they think of it? Leah was embarrassed. The walkers, the liver spots, the false teeth, and the blue hair told her this group could have no objectivity when it came to eternity. But the senior citizens began. They disagreed. "Fool," said one old man to the woman beside him, who was making angel wings with her arms.

"What does your soul rest in, outside your selves?" asked Ollie. "Where would you like it to be, if you could leave it behind you after you die?" he asked. Leah turned her head away. She was uncomfortable. She had no illusions about the soul. It was biochemistry, from molecule to molecule, she believed. As the senior citizens talked, Leah saw their eyes focus and their backs straighten. The answers came, "The ocean," "The lighthouse," "My azalea bush," "My granddaughter," "My boat" "A sea gull," "Madonna," said a thin lady with hair puffed like a winter dandelion and arms like twigs, "The windmill," "The dune grass," "The north wind," "My dog," "A horse," "A baseball."

Ollie said, "If you care for something you become a part of it, forever. That's what the poet said." The stale smell of age disappeared from the room. How, Leah wondered, did he do that?

She was nervous as he introduced her. What if she spoiled the mood? What if he didn't like the way she spoke? She felt excited, faint. She searched his eyes as she spoke. She wasn't used to talking to nonscientists, old nonscientists. She wasn't sure they understood her. She talked very fast. Too fast. She tried to slow down. She was too hot. She wanted to stop and take off her sweater. She kept going. He nodded to her, encouraged her with a wave of his hand. When she sat down, he whispered in her ear, "You were great. You're clear, really clear." Relief and pleasure roiled within. She smiled at everyone. Even Sally, who wasn't looking at her.

On the way back to her house after the evening's coffee and cake, Leah told Ollie that her father had been dead for two years. "I miss him," she said. Leah was quiet. So quiet that Sally, who had fallen asleep in the backseat, woke up.

Leah didn't invite Ollie and Sally back into her house. She said good night on her front steps. Ollie had walked her up to her door. "We need to talk," said Ollie.

"Yes," said Leah. He probably wanted to explain why he couldn't see her anymore. He was a kind man. He wouldn't just vanish without a word. She didn't want to hear his explanations. It was nothing. She wasn't the sort of woman who thought that sex entitled you to a lifetime of fun and games. She was in a hurry to get in the door.

Ollie said, "I'll be by tomorrow night." He waited for her to say she didn't want him to come. She didn't have to, after all. She might have gotten what she wanted. She might have no interest in him. Sex, even good sex, was no guarantee that a woman wanted you again. He was standing there not breathing.

"All right," she said.

"I wish," he said, "I could give you a present."

"I don't want a present," she said, confused.

"But I want to give you something."

"What?" she asked.

"Something as beautiful as you are," he said. Quickly, before she had a chance to respond, to wipe the startle out of her eyes, he turned away back to his car. Sally was staring at him, her face pressed flat against the back window, her nose mashed down, her mouth making a wet mark on the glass.

Leah Rose did not think she was beautiful. But she wasn't sorry that Ollie Marcus thought she was. She considered him carefully. His arms, for one thing. His chest for another. Wide with gray hair curling about. She thought about her own body. She stroked it kindly. She lifted her arms over her head and stretched up and down toward her toes, she felt the muscles of her body pulling. She smiled. She traced the outline of her mouth with her fingers. Some sensation remained, lingered there. An interlude, she said to herself. A temporary pleasure, like eating chocolate ice cream. It's all right, she said to herself.

She sat in her living room, cross-legged on the floor, and picked up a journal, *Cell*. She skimmed the first article. She felt a tension in her shoulders. She bent her head forward and rolled it around in a semicircle. Suddenly she felt far away. Far away from herself, as if she were in an airplane and her body was down on the ground, a spot, a small darkness on the surface. She closed her eyes. The distances grew, sky to earth, self from self. She curled up her legs against her belly. It made her rock from side to side. She felt alone. She put on a record and took off her clothes. Naked, she danced a slow dance that involved a lot of spreading of arms and tilting of head, flexing of muscles, stretching up toward the ceiling. It made her feel better. Later, well after midnight, she called the weather station for the latest report, hazy and sunny tomorrow, temperatures around forty-five degrees, it said. Then she fell into her single bed and, letting her hair out of its clip, stared out the small window at the starless sky.

Ahead of her on the beach Leah saw Dr. Sonnabend in his hip boots and his surf-casting rod. He was shaking his line up and down while reeling it in as if motion itself would cause a fish to swallow the silver lure. Each man had his own style of casting, like handwriting, character was revealed in the smallest of choices. Dr. André Sonnabend hopped up and down on the beach, he made circles with his boots in the damp sand, he kept staring at the waves as if will, concentration, begging, could bring him his fish, his fish that was swimming out there, too close to shore, too stupid to tell metal from matter, too hungry to look closely, devouring blindly without caution whatever was in front of its wide and rubbery mouth, ready to die. "Eat, eat," he said to the fish. The wind hit at his face and he felt the spray cold on his forehead. He dug his heels in and cast again. The fish, eyes glazed, gills heaving, lying in his bucket, would be a sign from above or below, a sign of his good fortune, of his prowess, of his own swiftness, of his selection among mortals. He wanted his fish. He was one of the many weekend surf casters who hadn't hooked anything for years, except bunches of seaweed, a jellyfish, and, one November day a decade back, a woman's blue jacket blown from the back of a boat.

The men of the town had trucks that went out on the sand and followed the birds, and they often came back with blues and bass and a gleam in their eye, a tale they told. Dr. Sonnabend, who came only on weekends, a psychoanalyst who sat in his chair and made interpretations Monday through Friday, he had no jeep with four-wheel drive to spin along the shore. He walked from the parking lot on weekends and he clipped fish recipes out of the *New York Times*, tarragon and coriander, cumin and ginger, lemon and fennel, these were his plans for the fish he would one day catch. His wife was used to it, the hours at the shore, the empty bucket, the shrug of his shoulders, next time, another day, who knows, it's bound to happen.

She spent her weekends taking long bike rides out to the state park and back. She soaked in the bathtub. She went to yard sales. She spoke on the phone to her grown children. She didn't believe in signs from above or below. He found this attractive. He was prone to drama. She was prone to silence. They suited each other. She slept long hours. He listened to Beethoven on his Walkman. She folded his underwear and his socks. He massaged the back of her neck. They knew each other's stories. He could anticipate her desires as she could his. They had met at the Lycée in Arles and made their way in time across the mountains to Spain. They had been young and the adventure was not all bad. They had made love in the grass and eaten berries pulled from bushes. She had wanted to be a painter. He had planned to be a jazz saxophonist. It didn't work out that way. He had gone to medical school in Albany. She had taken courses at the university. For the last twenty-five years they'd had adjoining offices. Their daughter had played the piano and their son had been on his school's chess team. He still liked the way his small wife curled her feet up under her, and she still liked the way he waved his fork in the air when he talked.

Leah spoke to André Sonnabend. The sea was roiling. No birds about. Not a good sign for fishermen. "Anything out there?" she asked. André was dripping water. He was pale. The wind was blowing the last strands of his hair forward over his forehead. He was jumping up and down and shaking his head as if he wanted to get water out of his ear.

"Leah," he said, "dear girl, dear girl." The words sounded above the surf, clear as a call to order in the court of final judgment. "Leah," he said, reeling in his line and coming up beside her. "The most terrible thing just happened to me. I must have had a dream, fallen asleep while standing here on the shore. I was fishing like I always do and I felt something take my lure, I pulled and reeled and it pulled back and it was huge and I needed all my strength just to hold on to my rod and my body jumped and surged with each pull. I waded out farther and the fish pulled me beyond the first sandbar. I was hardly able to turn my reel. I thought about letting go, but it's been so long, I wanted the fish. I held on. I found myself pulled out over my head and my feet were scrambling for the bottom I had lost, and I was frightened because I had on my boots and I could sink. I let go of the rod, because after all I'm not crazy, and just then a great mouth opened in front of me and the tide grabbed me and I was swallowed down the gullet of this giant fish, maybe not a fish, maybe a whale."

Leah shifted her weight and swung her arms across her chest. It occurred to her that madmen must be attracted to the profession of psychoanalysis, maybe they hoped to heal themselves. Maybe when they gave up hope of healing themselves they went mad entirely. She said, "What a strange dream."

"I'm not sure it was a dream," he said.

"Of course you are," said Leah.

"There's more," he said.

Leah sighed. "I'm walking," she said. "Perhaps next time you'll tell me what happened next."

Dr. Sonnabend put his hand on her sleeve. "Please," he said. "Listen."

Leah sat down on the sand. Dr. Sonnabend sat next to her.

"I was swallowed with a stream of water. I was wet all over. There was a smell of dead and rotting fish. It was very dark. I could see white bones along the side and a glow from the water, iridescent creatures created some light. I could breathe, I could see. The smell was terrible. The fish swam away from the shore. He dove deeper and deeper. My ears were hurting. I was treading water. I was holding on to his ribs so I wouldn't be shaken up and down. I pounded against his side, 'Let me out, let me out.' Down he went. 'What have I done to deserve this?' I called out. I felt a stinging on my legs right through my hip boots and I knew that the fish was digesting, some chemical process would soon turn me into a protein source. I yelled and I cried. I wanted my wife to know that I had loved her. Whatever, I loved her. I wanted my children to know that I wanted their happiness more than my own, more than anything. A dead eel slipped across my arms. I understood suddenly as if a light bulb went on in my head, like in the comics, I knew that I had disobeyed God. He had asked something of me and I had not done it. But what was it? I couldn't remember. The fish opened his mouth and more water poured in and I was floating and there was only room for my head above the water and I thought, Now, this is the moment I will die, and then I was back on the shore fishing just like I had been doing before."

"What a dream." Leah patted André Sonnabend on the arm. "We all have odd dreams."

"But don't you see," said the doctor. "I don't believe in God. I couldn't have had that dream. Also," he said, "even if God represents only my superego, or my former analyst, even then, what have I done to deserve such a dream?"

"I can't imagine," said Leah. "Are you overworking? Too many patients? It must be hard, day after day listening to other people's troubles." She rose to her feet. He stared into her face.

"The whale," André said, "he could be a representation of my unconscious rage, primitive fury that resides in the most reasonable of minds."

"I suppose," said Leah. "I'm reading *Moby Dick*," she added.

"Or," said André, "it is conceivable, someone might say, not me, of course, but it could be said, that I am the indigestible particle in the whale's belly. I am the primitive unconscious of the whale while he is the creature trying to simply live his life according to natural dictates."

"An environmentalist could say that," said Leah, "but it was just a dream."

"Or a hallucination," said André, shaking his head mournfully. "Or it was real," André added. He stood up, and taking his rod out from his stand, he cast again into the waters, wading out cautiously, only a few feet into the surf. Leah watched him for a moment and then walked on. He did smell oddly of dead fish, or something rotting. He needed a shower.

"I hope you catch something," she called out, but she wasn't sure if he heard her over the crash and slide of the surf.

Later Leah stopped by the Sonnabends'. Perhaps Dr. Sonnabend needed help. They were older people. He had helped her mother. She had a responsibility toward them. She put her bike in the garage and walked around to the back door. Inside the kitchen Dr. Sonnabend was leaning forward in his chair with his head in his arms on the table. Litzie Sonnabend was drinking a glass of red wine. They had a dog, a small hairy dog with buckteeth. It barked at the door until the Sonnabends heard Leah's knock.

"What I told you today," said André, "was exactly right. My wife thinks I've made it up. She thinks I am trying to torment her for some crime in our marital past. But I'm not. I'm trying to tell her that on the beach today I was pulled inside a whale and regurgitated onto the shore."

Litzie's hands were shaking. "I think," she said to Leah, "he might have taken a double dose of blood pressure medicine." She turned to her husband. "Did you feel dizzy before, did you have palpitations?"

"You've asked me that already," said André. "Do you believe me?" he said to Leah. Leah took off her jacket and reached down to pet the dog, who had not stopped barking.

"It is possible," said Leah, "that medical doctors, even psychoanalysts, even psychoanalysts who train other psychoanalysts, could slip in the mind, develop a Parkinson's, a phobia, a hallucination."

"Physicians have bad health too," said Litzie. Her eyes filled up with tears. The tears spilled down her fine cheekbones and onto her sweater. "I don't want our life to be over, not yet," she said to her husband. "Please," she said, "be sane." She held his hand in hers, some childish way, some flirtatious way, something out of the language of their marriage.

Leah stared. "I should go," she said.

"Sit down," said André, "we'll talk of something else. Your father," he said, "loved a good wine."

"I know," said Leah.

Leah told Ollie that night. They were sitting in the living room. Ollie had made a fire. The room was dark except for the glow from the logs. The light from the fire flashed across the Indian portrait, making the face less stoical, more threatening, more alive. Ollie had brought a bottle of red wine. "Imagine," said Leah, "going to a psychiatrist who thinks he's been swallowed by a whale. There ought to be some way to warn his patients."

Ollie considered. "Is the handwriting on the wall Freud's?" Leah laughed.

"He did smell of dead fish," Leah said.

"It's just the beach," said Ollie. "Every now and then the tide brings in that smell." Ollie was sitting on the couch, his leg touching Leah's. He felt heat from her skin right through her jeans. Or was it heat from his skin that was running up his thighs, causing spasms of expectation in his groin?

"Have you ever been to a psychiatrist?" asked Leah.

"No," said Ollie. "I've talked with several, about Sally," he added.

"Any help?" said Leah.

"No," said Ollie. He reached his hand out and stroked her hair. He touched her the way one might an angry child, his fingers hardly pressing down, his movements very slow, steady, calming. She stretched out her legs. There was silence. They both waited. They both wanted.

"Long ago I had a diaphragm," said Leah. "But I didn't use it very often and it cracked. I threw it out. I'm probably beyond conceiving anyway. I'm not so young."

"Neither am I," said Ollie. He put his head down in his arms. For a moment the years of his life weighed on him. Then he noticed the glow of the fire reflected on Leah's face. "Now," he said. "Just think of now."

Soon she was naked. Soon she was on top of him. Bone to bone, flesh to flesh, she felt herself expand, would she float up above him? She felt herself locked in the cradle of his hips. She pulled in air, she released it, she stroked his skin, she bit at his arm, she ran her hands against his chest. He pounded on, pursued, pursuing, escaping, captured, he ran, he surged, he slowed, he sped up, he sank, he kissed her mouth, he kissed her nipple, he held her close, he let her free. She pulled at his ears, she lifted herself above him, she fell down. If she were a glass she would shatter. She was not a glass. Sexual pleasure was evolution's device for survival of the species. Clever, she thought, brilliant, in fact, perfect.

Later he said, "Tell me about your parents."

She said, "My mother wasn't happy. My father wasn't happy because he couldn't make my mother happy."

He said, "That's all?"

She said, "It wasn't his fault."

He said, "I didn't blame him."

She said, "It's a long story."

He said, "I have time." He had forever, nothing he would ever want to do again but listen to Leah, lie with one of her legs looped over his, with his hands on her back, touching the slope of her shoulders, with the tips of his fingers he could stroke her hair, with his eyes he could watch her, watch her look away from him, back toward him, shift on her pelvis. He pulled the quilt up over her lap.

"I'm thirsty," she said. "Are you?"

"No," he said. He was content.

"I'll tell you later," she said. "Now isn't the right time."

Ollie let his body tip gently over hers. "What is the most terrible thing that ever happened to you? Tell me now." She opened her eyes wide and stared at him.

"Why should I tell you that?" she asked.

"You should," he said, "you should." She believed him. She told him about the time she came home from school and called her mother and her mother didn't answer. She paused.

"That's it?" said Ollie.

"No," said Leah, "that's not it." She took a deep breath. He was waiting. "Then I found my mother," she said, "standing by the window, looking down on the street. Her hair was shaved off her head. She had used an electric razor, there were spots she had missed. She was wearing her slip. She wouldn't speak to me. I thought she was dead, dead standing up. I went up to her and kissed her hand. It worked for Sleeping Beauty, I thought maybe a kiss would wake her. She didn't move. That's it," said Leah, "the worst thing."

"Was she dead?" asked Ollie.

"No," said Leah, "not really, not then."

Ollie had listened. He saw the little girl staring at the woman, the woman whom he imagined like Leah, with wide hips, a long oval face, and a tense pulling about the mouth. "Did she love you, your mother?" he said.

"Yes," said Leah.

"So tell me more," said Ollie. He had a deep voice, a kind of soothing rocking mellow voice, that suggested he could never be surprised.

"No," said Leah. "You tell me something." And he did. He told her about the way his father built a red wagon for Sally down in the basement. He told Leah about his mother's sister, his aunt Reba from Brooklyn who came once a month to visit, bringing blintzes and bagels and herring in cream, things scarce in West Pine. He told her about the penny he had put on the railroad track and the train coming fast and faster till it turned his penny into a large glob of smooth copper. A lucky penny. He made the sound of the train whistle. Leah laughed. He told her about the first time he was invited to a birthday party and he hadn't brought a present because his parents didn't know about birthday parties, not the kind they had in West Pine. He told her he was a bomb baby, born one year after Hiroshima. His father had been a submarine radio operator. Solomon Marcus reported that once he had cruised just off the coast of Montauk and his wife didn't know how close he was. Ollie would think about that as a child. His father there but not there, just under the waves, invisible but there. His favorite food as a child was peanut butter and jelly. Leah said hers was Sacher torte; Sacher torte, she explained, was a Viennese chocolate cake. Her father would bring it home in a box with a thin red ribbon just for celebrations.

"What's the worst thing that ever happened to you?" Leah asked. There was a long silence. "Can't you think of something?" Leah said.

"No," he said. Ollie turned to her, staring right into her eyes.

"No?" said Leah.

"Not now," said Ollie.

"It's all right," said Leah. "I'll tell you instead about my friend Myrna whose son, Danny, has a snake."

"Tell me all about her," said Ollie.

Boris called: "So, what are you doing these days?"

Leah said, "Fooling around."

Boris said, "Come back."

Leah said, "If you were a man, would you like me to be sexually aggressive or would you rather I waited for you to make the first move all the time?"

Boris said, "I am a man."

Leah said, "I mean if you were a man on a couch sitting next to me."

Boris said, "I'd like to make the first move and the second, but I like it if a woman makes the third or the fourth, after that it should be like a Ping Pong game, bounce bounce."

Leah said, "What if I drop the ball?"

Boris said, "He can get a new girl."

Leah said, "Thank you."

Boris said, "Don't get into trouble."

Leah said, "Boris, if you were a man, could you feel seriously about me?"

Boris said, "I am a man. But I have a girlfriend and you're

older and you're my boss and this is a weird conversation we're having."

Leah said, "No, I mean if you were a man I just met and you weren't involved with anyone but your sister and you seemed to be interested, would you be very interested or not?"

Boris said, "I could love you, Leah. All over the planet there are men who could love you."

"Really," said Leah.

"For God's sake," said Boris.

Sally was sitting at the table in the kitchen. She was petting Elijah, who arched his back and kneaded his paws on the folds of her stomach. She listened for the sound of her mother's voice. She did not hear it. She felt tired. Her body was bloated. Her stomach like a soft pillow, larger today than yesterday, and she was bleeding again. She knew it was all right. She knew it was normal for women. She knew what to do. Even before Mrs. Roomey had given her the pads she had known that it was all right. She knew that other women had babies because they had bleeding. Her mother had explained it to her. Ollie had explained it to her. She understood. She could not have a baby because she was not like other women, and babies needed regular mothers, not her. She sat at the table and her breasts felt full. There was a weight in her body, an ache that made her restless. She stamped her feet. The cat jumped off. She sat there. Mrs. Roomey said the TV was on too loud. Sally pulled herself to her feet and went over to the set and increased the volume. "Turn it down," yelled Mrs. Roomey. Sally pushed the up button. Mrs. Roomey came in the room. She turned the TV down. Sally looked out the window. She sat there. The cat jumped back in her lap and put his head down into her large hands. She held his head. "Sweet-heart," she said.

Ollie woke up and walked down the hall. Sally was waiting for him, all dressed, her sweater pulled down over her jeans. She wanted syrup for her breakfast pancakes. They walked into town. The chill air made him stand up straight, move fast, swing his arms. The cold made Sally's leg hurt. She pulled it along after her. Maybe he should have taken the car. The cold air made him remember he had to order more wood. The tops of his ears turned red. The leaves were dropping, blowing past. They reached the corner where a thicket of trees ran back as far as the railroad tracks. There was a sudden crashing noise. From under the bram-ble came a fawn. Looking not right or left, it ran across the road, directly in front of them, its white tail following, its spindly legs galloping. It disappeared behind the hedges of the Carstairs house. "See," said Sally. He did. For a moment the fawn left a trace of itself on his eyes. Hope bounded up in his chest. If only Leah had been with him. If only she could have seen it. He would tell her about it. He practiced telling her. He revised his description. If only Leah had seen the fawn. Then his morning would have been perfect.

Waking early in an empty bed, Leah saw the drops of mois-ture on the windowsill. Leah felt uneasy. She waited and listened for the sound of a car coming up the road. Then she didn't like the waiting, herself waiting. She put on her jacket and gloves and went down to the beach. She saw the sun, a hard gold eye, casting silver lines along the incoming waves. The sun had no warmth. A gray steam hung over the dunes. As she walked it slowly lifted and the sharp blades of grass turned a dusty green in the daylight. She heard the waves, drumming on the sand, and the caws of a gull. She saw a flock of lesser terns lifting off over the waves. Their voices scratched against the sky, like so many forks on a plate. She picked up a skate case, its black hard surface had been cracked and the eggs had long ago floated out. It looked now like a wounded bat, dried and dead on the sand.

She walked as close to the water line as she could, her boots leaving deep prints in the damp sand. She looked down and saw a starfish, perfect, encrusted with sand, drying on the shore. Its points had started to curl inward. Floating in the water, it had a red shine, here preparing to rot, it had become the color of mud.

Leah remembered. One summer, her mother gone again, she was sitting on their red and white blanket, under the fringed beach umbrella her father dragged down each day, with the Resnicks and the Birnbaums and the Adlers and the Adlers' new baby and the Fines' teenage daughter lying on a towel, a few yards apart, spreading cocoa butter on her limbs, and Mrs. Fine in a chair with a towel across her legs and zinc oxide on her nose, and Paul, who was Paul? Leah couldn't remember, a child her age, a child who was visiting. She was down at the water's edge with Paul and they were jumping over the remains of a castle, someone else's castle, they were indifferent to the survival of its walls. Leah had seen the first starfish and then another and then when she stood up she saw that they were all along the beach, starfish drying out in the sun. She ran back to the adults. "Why are they here?"

"A wave, a shift in current, an upheaval on the ocean floor, it happens now and then, nothing to worry," said her father.

"Starfish on the beach make good food for the birds," said Mr. Adler, patting her shoulder.

"No," said Leah, "they're not dead yet." She knew because she had picked one up, held it on the palm of her hand, and seen it twitch, felt its shape, known it was still alive.

"So," said Mrs. Adler, "leave them be."

Mrs. Birnbaum was heavy, her thighs were huge and pale. She pulled her bathing suit skirt down to cover them. "Darling," she said, "there're plenty more starfish where those came from."

Leah considered. "Papa," she said, "we have to save them." Her father laughed. Not a real laugh, just a sound. She had heard that before.

Mrs. Adler said, "Have a sandwich. Take a dime and go get an ice cream."

Leah ran to the shore and gathered up three starfish and then she waded out into the surf and threw as far as her arm permitted. The starfish splashed into the oncoming wave and sank down. Paul followed Leah. He threw his starfish after hers. Then the two children ran over the eddies of froth that marked the limit of the last wave and gathered more starfish. Save them, save them, Leah said to herself. "Help me, Paul," she called when he got tired and sat down. Don't stop, she said to herself when the muscles in her arm began to ache. "Save them," she called. It was no use asking the adults. They barely watched her. They had no interest. It was a game for a child, they thought. Except for her papa, who knew what she was doing. He followed her along the beach.

"There are too many," he said. "The next wave will bring them back in."

"Help me," she said.

"No," he said, "there's no point."

"There is," she said, "there is." But she could see that more starfish, replacing those she had thrown back, had already washed ashore. Maybe more were coming. Paul had had enough. He was eating a red Popsicle that was melting on his chin and dripping onto his chest. "The starfish are dying," said Leah, who still ran up and down the beach, putting the starfish into her pail and throwing them back into the sea until it was time to go, the air had turned cool and her father had packed up the towels and folded his chair. "There'll be more tomorrow," Mr. Birnbaum promised. But the next day they were gone. Only a few dead starfish that had washed up near the base of the dunes.

Her fingers were cold. She put them in her pocket. For the first time in years she yearned, for what? It made her impatient, angry even, this insatiable hole that had opened in her. What did she want? More, she thought, more and more. Her legs ached. Her muscles were sore. They had not been used in a while. She felt rumpled. She felt old. There was no one on the beach that she could see. A small muscle in her eyelid twitched on and off. Her hair blew into her face. The sand stung. She put her head down. There was fungus growing on a piece of lumber. Blue and green in a lace pattern, it climbed the top of the wood and disappeared into a dark crack. She thought about Ollie Marcus. Whatever else she started to think about she ended up thinking about Ollie Marcus. She thought about Sally Marcus. Why hadn't he found a home for her, a place where she could be among her own kind? She tried to imagine the chemical imbalance that washed Sally's brain. The structure of the cells that had gone awry. She felt a familiar surge of excitement. Someday, someone would know the exact chemical chain, the precise structural error. Meantime Sally was a fact. Sally's body was huge. Leah did not feel comfortable around huge people. The dimples in their arms, the flesh that hung, the stomach and the thighs like trunks of trees. Sally was more than fat. She was unshaped, unformed.

Leah considered: often things that were not going to work aborted. Creatures with three legs instead of four, with open spines or toothless mouths, cortices, limbic systems, shrunk or swollen, creatures that were useless and couldn't feed themselves died. She had studied with a chemistry professor whose collection of teratogenic fetuses in jars floated in formaldehyde in his dark supply closet, error preserved for the amazed eye of science. Normality, banality, ordinariness: what blissful words, what fine words.

What she was thinking was unthinkable: sorrow followed shame.

Her attention returned to Ollie. She imagined his wide back with the spine not absolutely straight. She imagined his hands, large, fingers running down her shoulders. She shivered with pleasure. She imagined his glasses sitting on her table. His eyes were watery, blue. They turned toward her, followed her across the room. He stared at her. She liked it. She thought about his corduroy pants, worn thin over the right knee. She was memorizing her memory of him. Searching for new details. Looking for ways to anchor the image firmly in her mind. If she never saw him again she wanted to remember everything clearly. Then suddenly she felt afraid. Afraid of being alone. Afraid that what had just come would go. Afraid that she had wasted too much of her life.

She looked down and saw a perfect scallop shell. Its ridges brown and pink, no holes at all. Its white surface hard, smooth, luminous, pure. She picked it up. She wanted to show it to Ollie. She wouldn't. Only children showed their shells.

Leah spoke to Myrna: "He's not my type."

Myrna said, "So what's your type?"

Leah said, "He doesn't know anything about induction, deduction, logic, neutrons, proteins, receptors. He's a scientific illiterate."

Myrna said, "That matters?"

Leah said, "We have nothing in common."

Myrna said, "So call it off."

Leah said, "How can you say such a thing, you don't even know him."

Myrna said, "You like him."

Leah said, "He's a diversion."

Myrna said, "You know, even though we've been friends since the Bronze Age, I have to say, you are one cold fish."

Leah said, "I'm not cold. I'm just scared."

Myrna said, "I know that. I wasn't sure if you knew that."

Ollie Marcus told his English class that Captain Ahab was not a man to succumb to peer pressure. "Anybody here want to be Captain Ahab?" he asked. The class laughed uncertainly. The ones who hadn't read the book, who were bluffing, who had asked somebody else to tell them the plot, who were looking for the movie in the local video store, they laughed too. "So you're afraid to be special," said Ollie, scornfully. The class was quiet.

"But he was crazy," said Ethel Pearce, whose own mother had embezzled from the bank where she had been a teller. Ethel Pearce had read the book.

Ollie said, "Crazy, mad, Looney Tunes, off the wall, bats,

nuts, out to lunch, that's right, isn't it. Aren't you glad you're normal. Normal as the day is long, normal as the color blue, normal is what?" Ollie stared at his class. There was an embarrassed silence. Ethel Pearce was staring at him. He changed the subject.

Myrna called her friend Leah.

"My stepdaughter is taking diet pills. I found them hidden in the laundry hamper."

"What are you doing about it?"

"Worrying."

"Confront her," said Leah.

"I tried."

"What happened?"

"She laughed."

"How's the snake?" asked Leah.

"Drooping," said Myrna. "The smell in the bathroom, though, it gets worse and worse. The super can't find the trouble. The plumber wants to replace some pipes but he's not sure the problem is in the pipes."

"Dig out the pipes," said Leah.

"I'm getting estimates," said Myrna. "When are you going to give up this hermit-on-the-ocean routine and come back?"

"Not yet," said Leah.

"So you're not such a hermit?" said Myrna.

"This man with the sister," said Leah.

"You did."

"Yes."

"Is anything going to come of it? Or is this another of your one-week stands?" said Myrna.

"I wish I hadn't started," said Leah.

"Why?" said Myrna.

"I hate waiting. I hate waiting to see what will happen next," said Leah.

"What's the alternative?" said Myrna.

"I want more. I could get greedy," said Leah.

"Sounds like the Bride of Science is ready for a divorce or a separation," said Myrna.

"A person doesn't have to give up science for sex," said Leah.

"You could've fooled me," said Myrna. "What do you think about my bathroom?"

"Try a room deodorant," said Leah.

The windmill at the end of town was propped up by a wooden structure of planks placed at angles every few feet around the base. The town was debating the cost of permanent repair. The Democratic head of the city council wanted to hire a local carpenter to complete restoration. The Republican majority on the committee wanted to permit demolition and then sell the land to a developer for a six-unit condominium. The windmill tilted to the left and the base was rotting. There was a dank smell coming from the structure that radiated out for a full hundred yards.

Ollie Marcus was addressing the town meeting on the historical importance of the windmill. Built in 1734 by the earliest settlers, it had been a home for butterflies, snakes, and red-winged blackbirds for many years. Once the floor of the mill had stored grain, once the great blades had moved the thresher and the mill itself had creaked and groaned.

Ollie intended to save the windmill. Leah sat in the back row of the town hall auditorium and listened to the rise and fall of his voice. She was flushed. She shifted frequently in her seat. She crossed and uncrossed her legs. She pulled at a frayed spot on her skirt. He spoke of the importance of history to the human heart. As he spoke, sparks came. He was, Leah thought, persuasive, lyrical. She might have lost her objectivity. No one in the room knew how well she knew Ollie Marcus. No one in the room had turned to look at her when he began to speak. She alone, in darkest secret, knew that the speaker and the woman in the back row had said and done things together that made them less than strangers, contingent on each other's person, a bleeding, if you will, of each into the other, of a sort that made his speech reflect on her and his words echo in her head unlike those of the speaker preceding or the one following. Suddenly she loved windmills.

Sally was sitting on a small folding chair next to Leah. She was rocking back and forth, tipping on the chair legs. Leah put out a hand to hold the back of her chair. Sally began rocking harder. She was making sounds, approval of her brother, "He, he, Ollie, Ollie," she crooned, at first softly, then a little louder.

"Sh," said Leah and gestured with her finger to her mouth.

"Sh," said Sally in imitation. Leah looked ahead of her. The people sitting nearby all knew Sally.

"Be quiet," said a man with a folded newspaper in his lap. When Sally murmured again he turned around and slapped his newspaper on the back of his seat. "Enough," he said in a fierce voice. Then he winked at Sally. "Be good," he said. She was quiet for a few moments. Leah took a deep breath. Sally shouted, "He has hair on his ass. Ollie has hair on his ass." She was waving to the people on the platform. Leah was pale. The man shook his newspaper at Sally. Sally was quiet. She blew bubbles with the saliva in her mouth. Leah tried not to look. Someone else stood up, an advocate for knocking down the mill and spending the money saved on computers for the elementary school. Ollie appeared at the end of their row and signaled Sally and Leah to join him. Sally rocked back on her chair and let it fall. Crash. A loud crash. Leah stood up. So did everyone else in the row. Sally wasn't hurt. She was laughing. The man at the mike asked if she was all right. She waved. They left the auditorium.

Leah in her car followed Ollie back to his home. "Sally will watch television awhile," he said. "We can talk." He brought Leah a glass of water from the kitchen, which still had the wallpaper that his mother had picked out, faded now, bunches of violets and dandelions in alternating diamonds.

"I'm sorry," said Leah when they were alone, "I couldn't keep her quiet."

"No one can," said Ollie. He shrugged. "She hasn't learned the rules, so they don't apply. She wants attention paid to her. She doesn't want attention paid to me. Her pleasures are her commands. She lets sounds out. She lets gestures fly. She follows some inner dictate. She is anticrowd, anticonventionalist, the individual marching to her own drummer. She'd march right in front of a car if I let her. She eats too much, she watches television till her eyes are bleary. She is the queen of excess, the madam of I won't." They had to shout. Sally had turned the sound on the television up higher. Ollie went and turned it down. When his back was turned Sally turned it up again. Ollie smiled, a corner of his mouth went up, his eyes asked a question, not of Leah. He bent his head. Leah's eyes invaded his privacy. They went into the kitchen. They still had to shout.

"Aren't you angry, about your speech?" said Leah.

"No," said Ollie. "There's no point in it."

"It was a good speech," said Leah. Ollie was pleased. He tried not to show it, like a man holding four aces in a high-stakes game.

"I can do better, even better," he said.

"Was she born that way?" Leah asked.

Ollie said, "My parents believed in the healing of time. My parents never gave up: 'Pick up your napkin, wipe your mouth, here is the globe, here is West Pine, here is a can of tomatoes, red is the color, blue is for berries, the large hand is the minute, the small hand is the hour.' " Leah could hear the adult voices, the rough edge of city sidewalks, railroad flats, fire escapes, and flapping laundry echoing through the house.

"And you?" asked Leah.

"I manage," said Ollie.

He showed her his desk. He showed her his high school picture. There he was in the center of the class, his ears sticking out, his hair dark and curly, something stubborn in the jaw, something amused in the tilt of his head, and his eyes, behind his glasses, gentle. Did he shave yet? His shoulders wide above a broad chest. Leah sighed. He looked so young, smooth-skinned, alarmed. Why didn't she know him then? She must have passed him on her bike in the summer. She must not have seen him. Leah walked around, not settling in the armchair, not lying back against the cushions of the old couch, worn at the arms, soft in the springs, not staying in the rocker by the window. She moved about, feeling unsettled everywhere. It didn't matter that Ollie was smiling at her, asking if the room was warm enough, that Sally was watching the evening news at full volume and loudly slapping her thighs. "What's the weather tomorrow?" Leah asked Sally.

"Rain, tonight, tomorrow," said Sally, who was twirling

her thumbs in some kind of lacy pattern, as if her fingers were crochet needles in her hands, as if she were tapping out the rhythm of the drops on the driveway, as if she were signing in the language of the deaf, a burble of vowels. Her tongue went in and out of her mouth, darting swiftly, rubbing sometimes against her dry lips. A bag of potato chips sat in her lap, a box of Entenmann's pineapple cake lay empty on the floor. She was rocking back and forth. "She does that," said Ollie.

"I see," said Leah.

Seated next to each other finally on the couch, they did not touch. Their knees were close. Ollie's drifted against Leah's but she moved away, not far, but far enough. Sally laid her head back in the chair. Her eyes were closed. Ollie turned down the sound.

"Was it a teacher," said Ollie, who always hoped everything good came from a teacher, "who led you to science?"

"No," said Leah. "It was my father who said everything wears a mask, look under the mask, don't be fooled. Don't wish, find out."

"He was a scientist?" Ollie asked.

"No," said Leah, "he worked for Mazine Dresses. He was a vice president. He didn't finish gymnasium."

"He must have been proud of you," said Ollie.

"Yes," said Leah. "He liked my smile. He said it was like his mother's."

"You knew your grandmother?" Ollie asked.

"No," said Leah. "Erased," she added. Ollie breathed deeply. Leah shifted her weight. She touched the brass base of the lamp. "My father," said Leah, "was not sentimental."

"I imagine not," said Ollie. "Mine was," he said into the pause that followed. "He liked Dick Tracy and Little Orphan Annie and he liked *The Honeymooners*. He bought glasses at the five-and-dime with pictures of Popeye and Olive Oyl on them. We still have them. You want to see them?"

Sally was snoring, a rasping sound rustled through her sinuses. Ollie and Leah walked upstairs. Ollie felt Leah walking behind him like a balloon he was trailing behind, the string in his hand. Balloons, he knew, were prone to bursting, suddenly, loudly. It was best to expect their departure. Ollie turned around and put his hand under her hair, tied back for the formality of the town hall, on her neck. She tensed the muscles of her shoulders. She felt his hand weighing down on her. Down in her belly, down at the base of her body from which fluids flowed and swellings came and went, she felt the tightening of parts long ignored, long forgotten, now newly tender. She moved away from his hand. "I have to go home," she said. She could see her car through the curtains of his window. Raindrops drizzling on the silver roof.

"I want to go with you," he said.

"You can't," she said. "You have to stay with Sally."

"I know," he said.

Later, when she was gone, hurrying out the door, bending her head down against the wind, holding the umbrella she had brought because the weather report had predicted showers, when her car door had slammed and he heard it start and the lights had flickered briefly against his outside wall, he stretched out on his couch and tried to read the paper. His eyes took in the letters but his mind ignored the words. He was agitated. He was distracted, his body sent him messages. His mind pushed them away. Leah Rose, her form, her silver loop earrings, her calves, her worn pink brassiere with the loose strap, her hair, her apricot shampoo, her bitten nails, her Seiko watch with the date and the time in all the zones of the world, her boots with the scuff mark on the left instep, the plaid wool skirt she had worn to the meeting, they all whirled in his head again and again. He blinked as if he could clear her out of his sight. He waited as long as he could. He called her on the phone. The line was busy.

Myrna said, "Be careful."

Leah said, "I'm careful."

Myrna said, "You're sure that he's not at risk. No drug habits, no prostitutes."

Leah said, "I asked but I can't be sure."

Myrna said, "What's his character flaw? Every man has at least ten of them."

Leah said, "I don't know yet."

Myrna said, "Find out."

Leah said, "I think he might be perfect."

Myrna said, "Yeah."

Ollie called an hour later. "I'm glad you came with me tonight," he said.

"I'm glad I did," she said. There was an uneasy silence.

"I want to see you. Sally has gone to bed."

"You can't leave her?" said Leah.

"No," said Ollie. "Can you come back?"

"Yes," said Leah.

The rain was heavy, pounding on the eaves when she returned. The newly fallen leaves clogged in the drainpipe made the water rush down in front of the window in Ollie's bedroom, a sheet of water. Leah and Ollie kept their voices low. Leah felt odd, illegal, wrong. "No, it's all right," said Ollie, "I'm allowed."

"But what if she comes in?" said Leah.

"She won't," said Ollie.

"Are you sure?" said Leah. She took off her sweater. She pushed it under the bed.

"I've never, here before, it just never happened. I never wanted it," Ollie explained.

Leah said, "I'm flattered."

Ollie said, "You should be."

Leah said, "It's like being a kid doing something with your parents upstairs."

Ollie said, "Don't feel guilty."

Leah said, "I don't."

Ollie said, "I do often enough."

Leah said, "Why?"

Ollie said, "It's normal."

Leah said, "Did you play baseball as a child?"

Ollie said, "I was just average. Nothing special."

Leah said, "You're not average."

Ollie said, "I wanted to be a poet. I was bad."

"Maybe not," said Leah. "Maybe," she said, "I'm making you up. You're a figment of my endless spinsterhood."

"No," said Ollie, "you're my dream girl."

"Bull," said Leah.

"What do you know about my dreams?" said Ollie.

"I don't like lies," said Leah.

"I won't lie to you," said Ollie. They whispered on. She sat naked on Ollie's childhood bed. It was small like hers. In the dark he put his hands on her navel. He put his thumb in her belly button. For a moment it frightened her. What if he went through the skin? No one had ever touched her there before. She laughed and he put his other hand over her mouth. "Sh," he said. With his thumb still in the center of her belly, he began to drum on her abdomen, a message of importance, an announcement of great joy to come. She leaned back against the wall and waited. She let him. She encouraged him. She moved toward him. She kissed his ear. He rolled over her. She let her tongue slide up his thigh. She discovered that she knew things to do that she had never been told. Perhaps she had seen them in the movies. She watched herself. She stopped watching herself.

Afterward she leaned her legs against his. She turned her body into a spoon against his spoon. He put his arm over her breasts. She was happy.

"Have you ever been to Paris?" said Leah, who was thinking of a particular cheese sandwich from a particular café.

"No," said Ollie. "I never left West Pine."

"Why?" said Leah.

"I couldn't," said Ollie.

"Maybe someday," said Leah.

"Not likely," said Ollie.

"Did you think about it?" Leah asked.

"What for?" said Ollie.

It was a shame to sleep, to waste time, but she drifted off anyway. He was happy. He sang in her ear, a song with a twang and a thump, something about a rednecked cowgirl who should take her boots and go. He was happy. He fell asleep too.

In the early hours of the morning, when the rain had slowed to a steady drizzle, after he had awakened Leah and she had left, closing the door quietly after her, he went into Sally's room and sat down watching his sister breathing heavily, tossing from side to side, kicking off the blanket he had pulled up. He thought about the time that he had come home from school and found his mother in the large green chair holding Sally in her lap. Sally was leaning against his mother, her head resting on her breast. Maybe she was six.

Her pants were covered with tiny giraffes and there was a red ribbon in her hair. Ollie had walked over to the chair. The afternoon sun was pale and clear. He could see his mother's face and he could see the spot on the top of her head where her hair was thinning and her pink scalp showed through. Sometimes she wore a scarf. She didn't ask him what had happened at school, what he had learned that day. She didn't ask him what books were in his stuffed bag. She didn't ask him anything.

"Living," she said, "it's a long time." What did she mean? He wanted to ask. He thought he shouldn't. He waited. "The angel of death," she said, "he takes his own time."

"Is something wrong?" he asked.

"You ask that?" she said.

He waited. "I mean today," he said. "Is something wrong today?"

"No," she said. "Everything is fine." He didn't like the way she said the word "fine."

"Everything is fine?" he repeated. She was silent. The boy approached the chair. His sister stirred. He moved away.

His mother said, "Fine." He went downstairs into the cellar and, sitting down on the hard cement, his back against the boiler, feeling it chug and churn behind him, he began to read. His father no longer worked at the bench he had kept in the cellar. His tools were rusted with dampness or covered with dust. The cellar was private. His father would never come there anymore. What book? Now he couldn't remember. How it gnawed at him, the things forgotten, memories partial and composite, memories that are outright lies and that hide other memories behind them. He puzzled. Why had that moment with his mother in the chair, that conversation, remained and why had it come to him now, not with new information, or startling discovery, but just the old mood, the same old thing, his childhood again, just as it had always been?

Myrna said, "Love?"
   Leah said, "I didn't say that."
   Myrna said, "Good sex?"
   Leah said, "Good enough."
   Myrna said, "So what's with the sister?"
   Leah said, "Oh God. She's large."
   Myrna said, "Well, that's not the worst thing."
   Leah said, "No."
   Myrna said, "He cares about her?"
   Leah said, "Yes."
   Myrna said, "Try."

Ollie sat in his car. The teachers' section of the lot was nearly empty. He was early. He leaned back and closed his eyes. Leah Rose, he thought, Leah Rose, Leah Rose, Leah Rose, Leah Rose, like a mantra the words ran one into another, the repetition went on and on. He said it aloud. "Leah Rose, Leah Rose, Leah Rose." He almost sang the words. He stopped himself. This was ridiculous. He began again in a whisper, "Leah Rose, Leah Rose, Leah Rose." He was late for class. All day it went through his head, A rose is a rose is a rose, a rose by any other name is a rosebush, rosebud, rose hose, rose nose, Leah Rose, Leah Rose, red rose, white rose, Leah Rose, nose, doze, Leah.

He came over to Leah's late Friday afternoon. Sally was in the truck. He was taking her to the duck pond. She had a bag of old bread on her lap. He invited Leah to join them. She declined. He had brought her a present. It was a weather radio. A small cube with a long antenna, it picked up weather reports from the coast guard twenty-four hours a day. "Thank you," said Leah. It was the right present. Sally leaned on the horn.

Ollie said, "I don't give every woman a weather radio."

Leah said, "I know."

Ollie said to his class, "The albatross is what?"

"A dead bird?"

"His sin?"

"The Holy Ghost?"

"Our sin?"

"What sin?" said Ollie.

"Under the Endangered Species Act, he could have gone to jail."

Ollie sighed.

Leah had dinner with the Sonnabends. "Your mother," said Litzie, "had the most wonderful clothes. In the summer we barbecued out at the beach, remember, your mother always wore a great hat and a long flowered dress."

Leah did remember. Once each summer toward the end of August, her parents' crowd had a party down by the ocean. Her father would dig a hole in the sand, the men would bring logs, and they would have a fire. The fat from the meat would fall on the flames and the smoke would rise up against the orange clouds. The children would jump off the high dunes. They would play games as the sky faded and the air grew colder. Leah was tall and strong. She chased the smaller children, "You're it, olley, olley in free." The sun, bloated and red, hung low on the horizon. Then Venus would appear, a pale dot to the left, and soon the sky would turn to milky blue and more stars spilled through the night and the air would get cold and the mothers would put sweaters on the small children and the spray from the ocean would make everyone's hair damp. The adults drank wine from paper cups standing by a card table, hauled down to the beach for the evening, covered with a cloth and bags of potato chips, bowls of salad, Mrs. Schrager's coleslaw, ketchup bottles, mustard and pickles. There were marshmallows for the children too. This was a custom brought to the picnic by the American-born children who had gone to camp in Maine and New Hampshire.

Later the adults sat by the fire and the children sang. The waves pounded. Above them a waning moon looked down. Leah had climbed to the top of the lifeguard stand. She could see all the way down the beach; fishing boats with tiny lights appeared on the far horizon where the earth sloped down. She thought of herself as significant, worthy. As if she were a coal glowing in the dark, intensely burning. Several summers her mother was unable to come to the picnic, and Leah and her father went without her.

Litzie Sonnabend said to Leah, "Your father was a handsome man."

"Yes," said Leah.

"He took good care of your mother. That must have been hard," said Litzie.

"Yes," said Leah.

André said, "I wasn't hallucinating on the beach. I am a very reasonable rational man with ordinary neurotic symptoms."

"I thought psychoanalysts were cured," said Leah.

"Like at Lourdes, you mean, where the crutches are left behind?" said André. "I was in the belly of the whale," he added.

Litzie said, "We've talked about this enough."

Leah said, "If it wasn't a hallucination or a dream episode while standing up, what was it?" André was quiet.

Litzie said, "You can dream standing up." She cut into her lamb chop and blood ran down the center of the plate. She turned to Leah. "Did your mother ever go back?"

"No," said Leah. "She couldn't."

Litzie said, "I've been back twice."

André said, "I don't see the point. Litzie goes there with her girlfriends. She thinks she must. I like to stay here in West Pine and go fishing."

Litzie smoothed her cropped hair. Her eyes were tired, watery even. Her hands had liver spots and at the back of her neck a widow's hump showed, pushing her head just a bit forward.

"The whale — ," he started.

"You had a dream, André," Litzie said, the way one glides over words that have been repeated too often, "either you fell asleep on your feet in the surf or you had a small stroke, a split second, a blood vessel broke. Now let's forget it." She smiled confidently at Leah.

Leah said, "It's over."

André said, "Maybe." But both women heard his reservation, his mask of politeness.

"Men are stubborn," said Litzie.

"Are they?" said Leah. She wondered if Ollie was stubborn. She wondered if she would ever get to know him well enough to know if he was stubborn. She wondered what his neurotic symptoms were. Had his poetry been really bad? She wished he were at dinner with her. She wished she could touch his hand under the table.

Later as André walked her to her car, Leah put her arm in André's. His chest seemed thin. Leah could see his shoulder blades underneath his flannel shirt. His arms were skinny but he kept himself in good condition. He worked out at a gym. "Upper-arm strength," he said to Leah, "that's what I need at my age to keep fishing." He said, "The Japanese are still killing whales."

"Yes," said Leah.

André smiled at her. "No wonder I don't leave home on dangerous journeys." Leah patted his arm.

"Do you think a man who lives with his damaged sister in the town they grew up in, in the house they grew up in, is off balance?" asked Leah.

"Depends. Without the facts, the inside-his-head facts, I can't tell," said André.

"How many times have you fallen in love?" Leah asked.

"Seriously about fifty times. Not so seriously about a thousand," said André.

"Not me," said Leah.

"You know how it is with dogs," said André. "There are dogs descended from wolves. They mate for life. They only love once. They have one connection in the world. Then there are jackal dogs who follow whoever feeds them. They love wherever they pee. They always are running around with their tongues out, licking any hand they can find. I'm a jackal, you're a wolf. Can't do much about it," said André.

Later that night she walked around her house, checking the windows for ill-fitted joints, checking the floorboards for cracks, checking the stove for a gas leak. She was hot and cold by turns. Was she getting sick, or was she restless? She felt flat, exhausted, dried, too old. She thought about calling Ollie. She didn't want him to think she did nothing but think about him. Don't think about him, she begged herself. What would be left in her mind if she took him out? This was the definition of heartbreak. Something that had never happened to her before.

Scientists did their best work when young. Had her moment passed? She listened to the late-night weather report on her new weather radio. Small-craft warnings, winds out of the northeast. Intermittent clouds and dropping pressure, turning cold in the late afternoon. When would Ollie come next? Would he come at all? Why hadn't he called in the late afternoon?

Leah's father had asked her, "Met anyone interesting?"

Leah had said, "Not really."

Her father had said, "I don't want you to be alone."

Leah had said, "I'm not alone."

Her father had said, "You never bring anyone home."

Leah had said, "When I'm ready."

Her father had said, "You met that biochemist at the Amsterdam conference. What was wrong with him?"

"I got bored," Leah said.

"You bore too easily," her father had said.

Leah had said, "You want to get rid of me?"

Her father had said, "Do you like women better, is that it?"

Leah said, "This is disgusting."

"You're too much alone," said her father.

Leah had said, "I have friends. I have fun, enough fun."

Her father had said, "Please."

Leah had said, "I'm very busy."

Her father had said, "Your friend Ming Ho from high school, she's had two babies."

Leah said, "I've published fifteen papers, I'm the senior author of five."

Leah's father had sighed. "What are you afraid of?"
Leah had said, "Nothing."
Leah's father had said, "Something."
Leah had said, "Bull."

She had gone with a girlfriend to a modern dance concert in a loft downtown. Someone touched the back of her neck. She felt a whirlwind pass over her. She turned around. The man in the seat behind her was gesturing to his male companion. He apologized for disturbing her. For months after she would remember the weight of his fingers and stop breathing for a second or two. At odd private moments in darkness, under the blankets, she allowed the man she had glimpsed in the loft, who had brushed against her, to lead her up on the stage and the two of them would perform a primeval tango for a wildly cheering audience. Then the image had faded, lost its power, she forgot about it.

Leah called her friend Myrna. Myrna said, "The snake is lying still. I think he's dying. We have to take him to the vet. Danny has hives from worry. What could be making that snake sick?"

Leah said, "Where did you get the last batch of mice from? Maybe they're contaminated."

"Oh God," said Myrna. "Spoiled mice?"

"Maybe," said Leah.

"Maybe my stepdaughter is poisoning the snake? Is that a terrible thing to think?"

Leah said, "Snakes have normal life spans. Snakes get viruses and cancers too. The snake may just be naturally ill. Nature doesn't get all fussed up when one snake expires."

"Danny does," said Myrna. "What's going on with you?"

"I'm waiting for him to call."

"You think he won't?"

"He will."

"Good."

"He's made a mess of my mind. I can't concentrate on anything else. I think too much about when he's coming and what he's doing and what he thinks of me and if he thinks of me at all and if I want him to keep coming, things like that. I know this is a disaster. This is the beginning of my nervous breakdown. I can feel it. I ought to go back to the city right away. Will you visit me in the hospital if I have a nervous breakdown?"

"No."

"What do you mean, no?"

"If you crack up because a man appears to be fond of you, tough on you. There are people in China, in fact all over the globe, who are cracking up for better reasons than that. I'll visit them all, a pilgrimage to every crazy house under the sun, before I'll visit you."

"Thank you for your sympathy."

"You're welcome."

"My mother," said Leah.

"I know about your mother," said Myrna. "That's no excuse."

"I wish you could meet him," said Leah.

"What does he look like?" said Myrna.

"Forty-three, curly hair, black and gray, glasses, big ears, wide chest, legs are a little bowed. He has a smile, sort of reluctant but gentle, very gentle. He has big hands."

"Not Arnold Schwarzenegger, but all right," said Myrna.

"He reads," said Leah.

"So do most of us over the age of five," said Myrna.

"I told you, he's an English teacher," said Leah.

"Is he a Democrat or a Republican?" asked Myrna.

"God, that hasn't come up. Democrat, I think," said
Leah.

"You hope," said Myrna. "Pro-choice?" she added.

"I suppose," said Leah.

"What do you two talk about?" said Myrna.

"Everything," said Leah.

"How interesting," said Myrna.

"I hope I have a few months. I hope it doesn't end right
away," said Leah.

"Do you know the average life span of a boa constrictor?"
asked Myrna.

Saturday morning: Ollie pulled up to Leah's house in his
pickup. He was alone. Inside his windbreaker he held something. He knocked on the door. A blast of cold air followed
him into the hallway. He pulled a book out of his jacket. "I
thought," he said, "you would like this. I'm teaching it next
week."

The Scarlet Letter by Nathaniel Hawthorne. Leah held the
book in her hands. "Thank you," she said. "I read it in high
school but not since. I'm still reading *Moby Dick*," she
added.

"I know," said Ollie. There was an awkward silence. She
didn't ask for his jacket. She didn't offer him coffee. She
waited. He thought about her body underneath her sweater.
He thought about her room with the doll's house on the
floor. He thought about her alone upstairs, making the bed,
turning on the radio to hear the weather report, walking
down the stairs. He thought of her like a cat left behind by
the summer people, roaming the house sniffing and rubbing, expecting footsteps, lights, food. He felt tenderness
and something else, something hard to push away, something that was not lust or desire, but rocked him anyway,

shaking his certainties, ruffling his habits, like today, when he should have taken Sally to East Pine to see the crafts fair at the Lady of the Woods parish house and instead he was here, at Leah's, his mouth a little dry, his ears red from the cold air and a thumping in his neck where his carotid artery was racing blood up to his brain at an unholy pace that might be killing him, even as he stood there.

"Will you have Thanksgiving dinner with Sally and me?" he asked. She hesitated. "I make a good stuffing," he said.

"The Sonnabends have asked me," she said.

He was silent. Disappointment beat against his skin. He felt sweat on his forehead.

"I'll come," said Leah. "The Sonnabends will understand." What was she going to tell them? She would think of an excuse later.

Ollie brought in some logs for the fire. Leah made them coffee. They sat down on the living room couch with its faded flower cushions smelling slightly of mold and salt. Soon they were naked. Ollie's hips pressed against hers. Would desire sweep away science or would it work like fertilizer on her scientific wit? She didn't care. Desire she had, urges she had, specific urges, "Here, touch me here," she said and he did, and she lay beneath him, lost in her own body's movements, its tides of filling and emptying, and she was grateful, not for the future or the past, but for the moment itself. Gratitude made her weak with eagerness, rocked her away with Ollie to places they had not yet explored together. It was a morning well spent.

In the afternoon they went for a drive some miles down the highway to a narrow dirt road that led past some small summer cottages into the national park, a nature preserve that stretched ten valuable miles long, five valuable miles wide, from the bay to the ocean. No houses had been built there. On the Atlantic side an abandoned coast guard station stood on rickety planks, its crow's nest tower stripped of paint, leaning backward as if to avoid the wind off the water. Down the road a hidden pond, with submerged tree trunks, sank into the hills, and beyond the pond began the walking dunes: no path, shrubbery, sand, berry bushes, tangles of leaves, abrupt parting of brush as rodent and snake responded to the shaking of ground caused by Ollie's and Leah's footsteps.

Ollie had come as a child, first on a school outing. Later he had come alone, leaning his bicycle against a tree trunk, moving into the quiet space, secretly. It was a good place for a boy and his private ambitions. He had hidden something there.

"What?" said Leah.

"A journal," said Ollie. "My first and last."

"What was in it?" said Leah.

"Everything," said Ollie.

"Where, where did you hide it?" Leah said.

"I don't remember," said Ollie.

Leah said, "You don't trust me."

"I was a boy," said Ollie.

"Still," said Leah. They came to the top of the dune and looked out at the bay, pale gray water, stretched ahead of them to the other shore. The slope of the island halfway across the bay looked like a sleeping giant, a shadow of a huge whale, and uninviting darkness. Sharp clear light filled the sky, and the water and the white sand appeared covered with ice, but that was only an illusion, the afternoon winter sun already on its downward course washed the whole visible world silver.

"There," Ollie pointed, and Leah saw the empty nests, twig and leaf, waiting for the return of the gulls, the terns, the sandpipers. In the spring they would come, lay their eggs, fly up in flocks, descend on fish flashing in the shallow water, unaware of the shadows circling above them, wait for their new generation, thousands of bird screams in the night. "Look," said Ollie and there on the pillars of an abandoned dock, once used by fishermen who had now moved off, become waiters or bus drivers, real estate men or carpenters, sat a dozen cormorants, their long black necks curled down against their chests. Several opened their wings and spread them out, black cloaks, opening and closing against skinny bodies, smooth-feathered, beady-eyed. Leah gasped. Above them a hawk circled, looking for dinner. Leah hugged her own body, feeling its shape beneath her bulky parka, her breasts were soft and warm. Ollie said, "Out here, in the summer, I once found a box turtle and took it home."

"Did you name it?" said Leah.

"No," said Ollie, "it died before I could give it a name."

"Oh," said Leah. She added, "I never had a pet." Why did Ollie find Leah interesting? Why did Leah find Ollie and his box turtle important? Why did neither of them think, as they looked into the bay, of Icarus falling from the sky, a little splash amid the busy canvas? Early love is surely the same as melting wings, flying high, too close to the sun.

Sally was at the Senior Citizens' Center. Ollie had left her there for the day. For Sally this was a treat. For Ollie it brought possibilities to Saturday. Many of the senior citizens gathered in the communal room, sitting at tables playing cards, grouped around the TV, sitting on sofas talking with one another, had known Sally all her life. They had known her mother and father. Perhaps not closely. In a small town differences matter, church and background, new and old, especially then, when if a house changed hands it would be known by its first owners' name for the next century. But most of the senior citizens had come into the hardware store, purchased a rubber mat for their bathtub, a washer for their faucets, a drainpipe for the roof, a rake for the yard, they had seen Sally sitting on a trunk behind the front counter and had nodded their head. Some would keep their eyes down. Some would smile. All knew what was what. They got used to her as they had gotten used to the Harris boy, who became paraplegic when tossed by a wave in his senior year in high school, and the child who lost his eye to a fishhook. It was only accidents, carelessness, drunkenness, fate playing jokes. Minna Howard's son had been born feebleminded and sent to an institution upstate. Gene Bartle's child had a birthmark that burned like fire across his face. Nina Parson's girl was deaf, so were the children of the chicken farmer on the road to East Pine, and the high school librarian had a shriveled arm. The town had its share of cleft palates and water on the brain and open spines. West Pine was not immune to the process of evolution, mutating genes not always offering improvement.

The senior citizens did not have time on their side but they still had time to be kind to Sally. They were, except for Rufus Wentzler, who never could remember who she was and didn't like the way she bounced around the room, her heavy weight leaning against chairs and her feet thumping too loud on the floor. He had his own concerns.

This Saturday Sally shared a bingo card with Mrs. Mellon, who had once been an accountant with the town tax department. Mrs. Mellon had recently lost her husband and was apt to let a tear roll down her cheek from time to time. Her mouth, however, was set in a smile. She did not believe in burdening others. She patted Sally on the shoulder when one of their numbers was called. She stroked Sally's cheek when she seemed too excited. She peeled the paper off the muffin with chocolate icing and a jelly bean eye that Mr. Schramm gave Sally. Sally hugged Mrs. Mellon, who let more than a few tears spill.

For Sally the day was good. The men and women who came and went in minivans, some in their own cars, some brought by their relatives, smiled and touched her, helped her to do things like open her napkin at lunch, unwrap her sandwich. They gave her candy and cookies and clapped when she sang a song for them that was her own version of the most recent Subaru commercial.

At three o'clock in the afternoon, as the November light faded, the elderly men and women who remained at the center got their coats and scarves from the hooks along the entrance wall, bundled up against the cold, and began to leave.

Ollie pulled up in the pickup truck, jumped down from his side, and moved as fast as a chunky broad man can toward the door. Sally saw him and waved. He had come on time. He took a deep breath and wished calm on his beating heart, his shaky legs. Sally turned toward him, her square face eager, her thrusting tongue hardly visible, her heavy body lifting itself forward as if in a skip or a trot. "I'm here," she said, "I'm here."

Ollie took her hand. "Of course you are," he said. "I'm here too." He smiled at her, their private smile, a greeting and a kiss combined, a touching of hand to hand, a locking of eye to eye, a way they were with each other that made other people fall silent and stare.

"My brother," said Sally, to no one in particular.

"Yes," said Ollie. "Brother," she repeated. She said the word carefully, pronouncing it clearly. Gently she ran her fingers over his morning-shaved cheek. Then she kissed her own fingers lightly. He had hurried. He had left Leah abruptly. He had wanted to stay.

Leah went to the supermarket. She saw a man in a leather jacket unloading a truck in front of the doors. She saw the curve of his body, the bend of his back, his legs tensed as he lifted a carton. Leah felt a throbbing in her body. She saw an older man with a checkered cap joking with the girl at the delicatessen counter. She saw him smile as he took his package. She felt a throbbing in her body. She saw a boy, a boy with a six-pack of diet Pepsi. His young face smooth and still unshaved. His walk included a sideways rock that spoke of swagger and hormone. He probably has his father's walk, thought Leah, and her body throbbed. This was new, this lustful dirtiness that came with her to the supermarket. She was awake where before she had been drowsing. She was newly gazing where before she had been indifferent. It was some form of compliment to Ollie, but of course she couldn't tell him that he had transformed her into a construction worker, watching the passing scene, issuing whistles from the sidelines, thinking unspeakable things, not exactly thinking them but responding as if they had been thought. As she wheeled her cart through the frozen food section, waffles to the right, vegetables to the left, and ice cream at the end, she considered that she had missed much. Too bad, she said to herself. She didn't feel bad at all.

The leaves had fallen. They were in a pile in the front yard. The first frost had come. The pipes in the house had rattled and burped but the heat rose, as best it could. In the bathroom the windows were iced over and there were mice droppings in the kitchen cupboards. Ollie sat waiting to take Leah to the movies. He had hired Mrs. Roomey. It cost double in the evening. He didn't care. Mrs. Roomey did not like evening work. She agreed out of pity. She pitied Ollie Marcus. Leah came downstairs in her jeans and a heavy sweater. He saw her profile at the base of the stairs. Her long hair moved with her forward, toward him. His wide body startled. He wasn't entitled, not to the urge that beat at him, not to the gentleness that rolled over him, not to the smell of her soap, not to the heat that warmed his gut, leading it to pleasure and peace in equal quantities, in huge quantities. Later they went to the Empire Garden restaurant down the highway. The smell of scallions and soy, oil and noodle, rose between them. Napkins were stained. They ate enormous amounts. Hunger was sated more than once. The fortunes baked into their cookies warned of investment mistakes and lost friendships. Ollie crumpled the slips of paper up and dropped them into his tea. Happiness, peace, luck, grace, forgiveness, that's what the cookies had meant to say.

They decided against the movies. He took her to the couch in her living room. It smelled still of mothballs. He made her a fire. He read her the poems of Hart Crane.

"What," she said, "I'm not sure I get it."

"That's all right," he said, "just listen." She stretched out her arms and he let her take the book away.

André and Litzie Sonnabend went to dinner at Mackie's on a Friday night with Leah. The Sonnabends had left the city early so that their country weekend would be long and restorative. They looked tired from the drive, which had taken longer than expected because of road repairs on the highway. Litzie complained. They had listened to whale songs on the tape deck all the way to West Pine. "Belugas —," André started.

Litzie said, "We agreed. No more whales."

André said, "I'm going fishing tomorrow. The *Blue Fin*, takes people out, costs a lot but why not. We're going out to the point beyond the lighthouse. It's a good time for blues and maybe even a tuna."

Litzie said, "Just fish, don't dream."

Leah said, "Enjoy."

André said, "A man has to think about his own death, imagine it, prepare for it, know it intimately before it comes. That makes him brave."

Litzie said, "It can make him morbid and nutty."

Leah said, "I'm interested in someone."

Litzie said, "The teacher?"

André said, "Good."

"Maybe," Leah said. "It's not so easy," she added.

Litzie said, "What isn't easy?"

"Thinking about somebody else all the time," said Leah.

"Oh, that," said Litzie. "You get used to that."

"He could change his mind," said Leah.

"So could you," said André.

"I don't think so," said Leah.

"Are you happy?" said Litzie.

"No," said Leah.

"That's a good sign," said André.

"Time is moving slowly. I need to know how this turns out," said Leah.

André said, "Take up fishing. It teaches you patience. I'm a very patient fisherman."

Leah said, "I'd like another glass of wine."

André said, "Sometimes every time you throw your line out you reel in a fish, most of the time it just sinks out there waiting, bobbing, nothing."

The food came.

*   *   *

Leah woke in the early, predawn hours. The stars were everywhere. The moon was round and white, slipping toward
the far horizon. Her feet were cold on the wooden floor. She
pressed her face to the cold windowpane. There was a crescent of frost near her chin. She wished he were in the house.
She wished he were in her bed. She wished for the comfort
of his legs wrapped around hers. She wished for the dent of
his body on her mattress. She sat in the chair and pulled the
blanket around her. She was awake. If she leaned her head
back far enough she could see the Milky Way, fading now,
dead stars sending their waves outward, afterthoughts,
ghost light, particles free-floating into her sight and out.
Leah longed. Leah wanted. Leah considered Ollie. She considered his blue cardigan sweater. It seemed to her there in
her chair, looking out her window at the night that hung
over the ocean, a beautiful thing, his sweater, its cable
stitch, the arm that it covered, the muscle and the tissue and
the hand, square, short fingers, a vein showing above the
wrist that extended from it, and the digits in the fingers,
and the nerves that passed through, and the worn wool of
his sleeve. She sighed. She was awake with anticipation, but
of pleasure or pain?

It was now dawn and the sky was pink and gray. Orange
light spilled over the sill and onto the floor. Leah had fallen
asleep in her chair. She woke with a small jump of her nervous system, as if she had been falling, as if she had been
shocked by a wave of electricity. She got back into bed. She
lay there, her eyes open, aware of the dangers of sleep. She
thought of André, who must just be getting out of bed and
putting on his thermal underwear, preparing his thermos of
coffee, preparing to go to sea and catch a tuna. She thought
of Litzie, her gray hair pressed close to her head, her face

washed of consciousness. It was hard to imagine. It is hard to imagine other people asleep. She thought of Ollie and drew a deep breath as if to counter the pressure in her chest, the weight of it, the dread of it. She thought of Ollie and wanted to do something, something for him, something that would ease him, something to make him smile, his quick pleased smile. What could she do? She wanted to be his angel of mercy, his vision of loveliness, his adventure, his journey, his travel companion, his friend. What could she do? Nothing came to mind. She nearly cried. She could feel the tears coming. She stretched out her arms and her legs. The morning was cold. She put on an extra pair of socks and a sweater over her nightgown. She saw a gull sitting on the roof of her neighbor's house. It dropped something down into the garden, a shell? An indigestible piece of scallop, crab, some formerly living matter? She watched the gull, its orange beak with its black spot on the end twitching back and forth. Her room was crowded with Ollie, his absence and his presence.

She closed her eyes. Maybe this was the kind of moment that brought inspiration, neutron and protein, helper arms and cell binding, she wanted to see something new.

Nothing. She had been right. A scientist should not have a flesh-and-blood man rumbling through her mind, taking up space. But she kept him there, going over the story of yesterday, moment by moment, as if she were rehearsing it, sealing it into her memory, as if it might slip away if she didn't make a special effort to delay its slide into the memory bank of other, more ordinary days.

Boris said, "You still seeing that fellow?"

Leah said, "Yes."

Boris said, "I thought you weren't interested in domesticity."

Leah said, "I'm not."

Boris said, "So what are you doing with this school-teacher, leading him on?"

Leah said, "Maybe."

School was in session. The day was crisp and clear. Ollie had an hour and half before his afternoon class. He met Leah at the beach. They sat down near the dunes, far from the surf, avoiding the wind. The beach was empty as far as the eye could see. The horizon was smudged in cloud. Leah dug in the sand with her fingers. A hole, a sloping-down hole. Ollie watched her. He began a hole near hers. He dug quickly. He dug with his fingers cupped, sand flying, he was making a tunnel toward her. She was lying flat on her stomach, her chin almost in the sand, she was digging. He was digging. He could put his arm down his tunnel. She could put her whole arm down her tunnel. She broke through a barricade of damp sand and touched his fingers. They couldn't see each other's hands. They couldn't see their own fingers. The tips of their fingers touched, under the sand the hands grasped each other. Ollie shouted, "I got ya, you can't get away."

"The hell I can't," said Leah, but she didn't move.

Ollie jumped up. He pulled Leah to her feet. Into the car. In the backseat, he kissed her face, her sandy hands, her thermal undershirt, her wool socks. He took everything off. His tie was flung across the steering wheel. They tumbled together on the seat. "I'm cold," said Leah.

"Not for long," said Ollie.

"What if someone comes?" said Leah.

"I don't care," said Ollie.

"Exhibitionist," said Leah.

"Lover," said Ollie.

Later she said the word over and over, lover, lover, lover.
Hers.

Thanksgiving meant that the stores had pumpkins in the
windows. The market had cutouts of turkeys hanging from
strings over the fruit bins. The black and white sign in front
of the Methodist Church said, "Thanks again, God." The
Reverend Sprool, 10:15 Sunday. The penny candy store was
offering chocolate turkeys. The West Pine elementary school
was having a costume party at which a member of the Shin-
necock tribe was going to present to the children a talk,
called on the note sent home to the parents "One Man's
Cooked Turkey, Another Man's Cooked Goose."

Ollie taught his last class before the holiday, his ninth-
grade English. "The moral?" asked Ollie.

"Bad luck follows bad luck," said a boy with his head
down, a kid who knew about bad luck.

"Maybe," said a student with braces still gleaming, "the
albatross is a symbol for the bride and the poem is a warn-
ing to be kind to women."

Ollie smiled. The poem would survive their interpretations. They would survive his efforts. The nasty gale winds
of guilt, the aftermath of wrongdoing, had not reached their
adolescent shores. So much the better. He let them go early.

At the elementary school the Indian representative of his
tribe spoke of the terrors of smallpox, the exile of peoples
away from ancient burial grounds, the starvation of children
on long marches to reservations, the old customs violated by
the white man's drink and guns, the massacres of animals
and men. He spoke of his grandfather who described the
osprey nesting in a field where the IGA and its parking lot
now stood. He spoke of the fish that were taken from the
bay, taken from his people. He talked in a low voice. The

kids in the back of the auditorium had a hard time hearing. He wasn't wearing feathers. He didn't play a drum. He wore no beads. "I am a remnant," he said, but the kids didn't know what a remnant was. The teachers were glaring at their pupils, be polite, be quiet, stop kicking the seat in front of you. When he finished, the second grade put on its play in which the girls were dressed as Indians and the boys were Puritans and at the table set up in the middle of the stage a child dressed as a turkey gave the final line, "Gobble, gobble, gobble."

Mrs. Roomey prepared the turkey the day before. Ollie had nothing to do but turn the oven on early in the morning. Leah made a sweet potato casserole and brought it over. Sally was wearing a long skirt and a pink blouse with ruffles over her breasts. Sally was excited by the preparations, by the holiday, by the guest. She hugged Leah when she came in. She held Leah's hand tightly in her own. Ollie sat at the head of the table and carved the turkey. He looked at Leah, his eyes filled with the suggestion of tears. He was pleased she was there. He was caught in a rare moment of contentment that did not depend on the moment that would follow. The sensation in his chest was of warmth, and comfort, rimmed by a shiver of excitement. It was a tenderness toward Leah, her body, her speech, her arm gesturing upward as she talked, her legs that touched gently against his under the table, her single strand of pearls that she had worn to honor the invitation, the day, her sense of rightness and fitness. Her hair was newly washed. In her dress, the one she had last worn to a site visit in Washington, she looked both older and younger, more of an adult in outer appearance, more of a child dressed up as an adult. Ollie noticed this without noticing it. The wave of tenderness that came over him when she stepped into the house, the wave that was over him still, through the dinner, made his lips feel full, and his foot tap the floor in a mixture of anxiety and joy.

Dinner was not entirely easy. Sally made noises, dropped her spoon, rocked back and forth in her seat. When Leah turned to Sally and asked her about Elijah, complimented her blouse, and admired the crayon drawings that were hung around the kitchen walls, Sally smiled and nodded. But when Leah turned to Ollie and asked him if Melville had a wife, Sally got up from the table and turned on the television in the living room. Ollie went and brought her back to the table. When Ollie asked Leah about her friend Myrna and the dying snake, Sally loudly hummed a song, one whose tune was elusive. Finally they ate in silence. Leah didn't mind. She understood. Ollie was embarrassed. Even knowing better, he had anticipated a meal with conversation, an ideal of holiday, one that he knew was unreal, even as he imagined it.

Later, when Sally was sitting in front of reruns of the Macy's Day parade and he and Leah were in the kitchen washing the dishes, he ran his finger down Leah's nose. It was a strange gesture, one that claimed more of her body, one that reminded her she had been a child and was now a woman, one that made Ollie dear to her, established their dearness to each other. It was better than words. Desire made her skin warm and she flushed red.

Ollie said, "Usually on Thanksgiving we eat alone. Sally is not used to company."

Leah said, "I go out. I've gone to Grossman's house in Connecticut. He's the lab head. He has a family. I know he's glad to have me. Everyone is polite. Politeness can make you feel extra."

Ollie was standing at the sink. He had taken off his jacket and rolled up his sleeves. His arms were in soapsuds up to the elbow. He wiped his forearm across his face, covering himself with suds. He was distracting himself from the image of Leah, alone at a table with others. It seemed to him suddenly that she was more singular, daring, unusual, better than anyone he had ever known. This of course he also knew was illusion. She was mortal. Her feet were clay, her heart was cracked, her pores were large, her body ached, there was gas in her belly, she was normal. He knew it, but he didn't believe it. He wanted to say, Never eat at a table without me again. He wanted to say, Whoever made you feel alone should die of boils, a ruptured hernia, or toothache. He wanted to keep her out of harm's way, under his wing, in his pocket, away from the wind and the ice and the looks of others. Her face, where the flush was draining and the color was returning to its usual hue, her face tempted him to believe that bliss was possible, at least for a moment stolen from some eternal clock.

They watched football. The large men in jerseys turned to the panning camera. "Hi, Mom," they waved; they mouthed, "Hi, Mom," one after another. Sally waved too. "Hi, Mom," she said to the TV. Ollie's team was losing. He explained it to Leah. She understood. The announcers bantered back and forth, the teams moved back and forth, first downs were ten yards, the idea was to get into the end zone. The other side had the ball. Ollie got upset and walked to the door, turning his back on the set. He closed his eyes. "I don't want to see this," he said. "I can't watch this," he said. "Fail, you bastards," he said.

"Turn it off," said Leah.

"No," said Ollie, "not yet. Maybe a miracle." There

wasn't any miracle. He looked miserable. "Fuck 'em," he said.

"It's just a game," said Leah.

Ollie said, "It's an important game."

"Next time," said Ollie a few minutes later and he smiled at Leah. It was a wide-open smile, dearness and gentleness, newness and joy, all the best possibilities in this best of worlds, flickered across his face. He smiled at Leah and she smiled back.

Saturday morning of the Thanksgiving weekend André Sonnabend, wearing his lumber jacket, his blue corduroy pants, and his sneakers, went out on Captain Michael Polsky's boat, the *Blue Fin*, looking for tuna. The large tuna, swimming deep in the cold water, could be found miles out to sea. You had to ride, bumping, sliding from side to side, crouched over to avoid the wet spray, for three hours out from land to the tuna fishing grounds, which the fishermen like their fathers and their fathers before them had learned were a good spot. Why there, André wondered, why not an hour closer to shore? Why did the fish swim in the same channels where the boats came day after day? If fish were people, one would speak of a collective wish to die, of maladaptive postures, inbreeding, mass retardation. As it was, André respected the tuna, they so often avoided his line, they so often pulled deep and, circling the boat, cut themselves free on the propeller edge. The tuna had their own methods of survival and André's concern was victory. "Goddamn fish," he would mutter, his eyes glowing with pleasure, his body leaning against the pull of his rod.

It was the one place, out on the water, with the waves slapping the side of the boat, with the fish deep below and the cold air stinging his not-yet-shaved face, salt clinging to his mustache, that André felt that he didn't have to listen, he didn't have to watch, he could let himself go, all for himself, into the act. His unconscious would, ignored for a while, bide with him, his conscious mind would focus on the tension in the line. He prayed for a fish and he didn't believe in prayer. He was over sixty-five and the back of his neck often ached, but his concentration, his power to will the fish to take the lure, that had to be better than ever.

Captain Polsky's radio was sputtering but there was a lot of static and the words were unclear. The postdawn sky was gray and dim, no glow of sun, no rose of the day, no fading moon, no sliding stars, just gray above and gray below. The waves swelled higher, the boat rocked. Captain Polsky and his crew, Jimmy and José, put on life jackets and gave one to André, who tied his, loosely, impatiently. He was fishing, after all. The winds were stronger. A storm, all unexpected, not predicted, was stirring, a squall from the northeast, not noticed by the coast guard, which had predicted drizzle and calm. The sky darkened. The boat slapped back and forth on the sea. "We're going back," said Captain Polsky, who was a cautious man. André was disappointed but he wasn't a child. Safety first, he told himself. Next time, he swore at the invisible tuna, next time I'll get you sons of bitches. He raised his fist.

It was hard to turn the boat around, the motor roared and clunked, the wind pressed hard. Jimmy and José were holding on to the sides of the boat and hunched their bodies over their knees. Captain Polsky, protected by the wheel, turned as hard as he could, a wave rose just as he veered right and washed over the boat. It picked up André, whose fingers lost their grip on the side, and pitched him overboard. His cry was swallowed by the dark and undulating water. His orange life jacket brought him quickly to the surface, and gulping water into his throat he screamed, "*Aidez-moi,*" the language of his long-forgotten childhood.

His life did not flash before his eyes. His thoughts were of Litzie, who would grieve for him, his thoughts were of his Monday patients, who would arrive at his door to find their doctor gone to the sea, his thoughts were of his mother, who had warned him once on a tour boat on Lake Como, Don't lean over the edge. His legs were numb with cold. He bobbed in the waves. His heart would go soon. His ears hurt. Let it end, he thought, every man must die. He thought of whales. He thought of large jaws opening and the rush of water swallowing him. His teeth hurt in his mouth. His chest ached as his heart squeezed on. He gulped air between the upward and downward slides of the wave. What was wanted of him? What had he yet to do? Why had he ended in the cold furious waves? He smelled brine, a tangle of seaweed, red algae floated against him, slapped him across the mouth, pressed against his jacket. Where the hell was Nineveh? Was he delirious? He wanted to be conscious as long as he could. When down to the last seconds, each second of mind alive mattered. He steadied himself. He would not die mad. He had not lived mad. With sanity came fear. He thought of sharks. Not that way, he pleaded, and he saw himself with bloody limbs, sinking. "*Chère amie,*" he called out to his wife. He stopped shouting and drifted in the storm.

Captain Polsky was shrieking into his radio, calling the coast guard. "Shit," he screamed at José, who was huddled at the bottom of the boat asking forgiveness from what appeared to be an endless list of women who had been left behind in Colombia. "Watch it," he yelled at Jimmy as the bait box slid out from under the seat and banged against the hull. The wind died down for a second, the boat rocked less violently, Captain Polsky saw André not far off the port side. He cut the motor, he threw a rope and André reached for it, and old man that he was, wet and cold as he was, he was hauled, by a now-restored vigorous José, assisted by Jimmy, onto the boat. He lay there, red algae on his arms and in his hair. His skin was gray, his eyes rolled in his head. He said to Jimmy, who offered him coffee from his personal thermos as they headed back to shore, "Am I lucky to be saved, or was I unlucky to have been washed over? Which is it?" "God knows," said Jimmy. Jimmy gave André a cigarette, which André took. He had given up smoking fifteen years before but perhaps that hadn't been necessary. Now André had the shakes. His limbs bounced up and down outside of his control. Had he damaged his nervous system? He trembled on and on. Captain Polsky was surprised at the smooth windless sea that followed them back to shore. "Storm passed through like it was never here," he said. "Never seen anything like it," he said. He glared at André. A gnawing fury grew in his belly that the word would get out, his boat unsafe, his customers avoiding him, chartering out with his competition.

André was trembling too hard to drive away from the dock. He was wearing a blanket that smelled of fish scales and sitting on a bench in the clam house with a cup of broth in his hands when Litzie arrived, driven by Leah. They had brought dry clothes. Litzie was breathing hard, like a woman who had raced miles along the road. "Why weren't you holding on?" she said.

"I was," he said. "There was a storm." Litzie looked out at the ocean, where the sky was now pale white, the sun rays coming sharply through the remaining clouds. At the edge of the horizon she saw blue.

"Yes," she said. Leah helped André into the front seat of his car. Litzie at the wheel considered widowhood. "Not yet," she bargained with whomever one bargains with when there is no one to bargain with, "please not yet." When he heard his wife's voice, tears came. He didn't want her to see. He closed his eyes, he turned his head away. Next to Leah on the backseat, André's wet lumber jacket was staining salt and water on the leather cushions. Litzie said, "André, was it an accident?" André sat up straight.

"How dare you?" he said. He was silent. Litzie put her hand on his shaking leg. He touched her hand carefully, just brushing the top of her leather glove.

Litzie sighed. "We should get a new car with an air bag," she said.

"Too expensive," André added, thinking that a good crash would be better than another toss into the sea.

Leah said, "Were you afraid to get married?"

Myrna said, "Yes, each time."

Leah said, "Really?"

Myrna said, "You think I'm dumb or crazy or what?"

Leah said, "Impulsive."

Myrna said, "Not you."

Leah said, "Not me."

Myrna said, "Lucky you."

Leah said, "Have you read *Moby Dick*?"

Myrna said, "Oh God, that book."

Leah said, "I like it."

Myrna said, "You've been brainwashed."

Leah said, "You only read junk."

Myrna said, "I like junk."

Leah said, "You should try *Moby Dick*."

Myrna said, "Boring."

Leah said, "You should hear Ollie talk about it."

Myrna said, "I worked all night redoing the face of the child in my divorce book."

Leah said, "What was wrong?"

Myrna said, "She didn't look miserable enough."

Leah said, "You should be able to draw miserable."

Myrna said, "Yeah."

Ollie talked to his sophomore class. He saw his students, each one blurred, as if the class portrait had been out of focus. He leaned against his desk. He felt vowels and consonants rumble far down in his throat and float outward. His mind was elsewhere. They were discussing Anne Frank. "Was she right?" he asked. "Do you agree with her that at bottom people are basically good?" The class was embarrassed. "Of course you agree," said Ollie.

He wanted to point out that Anne Frank was whistling in the dark to keep up her courage. That she made her statement shortly before she was caught in the carnage that demonstrated for all time the opposite point. But the faces before him, they didn't want to hear that. The acne and the excess pounds, the drumbeat of loneliness that lurked in the corners of the room, the girl whose father had left forever, the boy with a stutter: they didn't want to hear that. He wasn't going to say it, not aloud. Let each of them find it out alone, and then deny it, deny that they know it. Ollie sighed. Martha raised her hand. "It's my all-time most favorite line," she said. "Anne Frank was so wise."

Ollie always taught the diary just before the Christmas break. It seemed to heighten the festive mood. This year even he was feeling excited. Not about the Christmas present exchange, or the annual faculty potluck dinner at the principal's home, but at the free time coming, time when he would drive to Leah's house and have breakfast with her, time when they would walk to town to buy a newspaper, time they would spend wrapped together by the fire he would make, time he would use to tell her the curios and the artifacts of his life, the still hidden and the surprises he had himself long ignored. The worth of his life, the sum of his parts seemed better in the telling. Now it had significance. When Leah listened he felt attached, not to her, although that also, but attached to himself. He wrote the assignment on the board. He hummed to himself. "Hark the Herald Angels Sing." Who cared if the Messiah was true or false, this was the time to be jolly, let every soul adore Him, "adore" was just the right word for the way he felt. Holy night he understood. Angels on high might or might not be watching, but holy he understood, holy he felt in his body, holy was woman, and woman was Leah.

Leah noticed that the coffee she had poured for herself had spilled onto the carpet. The carpet that her mother had said was stain-proof because it was patterned with roses and leaves. Who can tell if something spills in a garden? her mother had said.

Leah said, "Do you still think about things your mother said?"

Myrna said, "Never." She sighed.

Leah said, "What's wrong?"

Myrna said, "The snake died. The vet did an autopsy. Can you believe it, an autopsy of a snake?"

Leah said, "So did he die of old age?"

Myrna said, "No, Drano, that long belly all lined with Drano. Danny won't let us take the empty cage out of his room. It's like a snake shrine or something, just sitting there."

Leah said, "I had a turtle that I put on the porch and it fried in the sun."

Myrna said, "I bet there's a residue of Drano under Sheila's fingernails. I bet she did it."

Leah said, "Did you ask her?"

Myrna said, "She denies it. Her eyes well up with crocodile tears. Richard says she wouldn't but I know it, she would. She did."

Leah said, "Forget it. You can get him another snake."

Myrna said, "Any other suggestions?"

Leah said, "He can't stay all night because of his sister."

Myrna said, "So see him in the afternoon."

Leah said, "I do."

Myrna said, "My bathroom still smells. It's been months. Richard doesn't smell it. Men have no sense of smell. The whole world could be a toilet, they wouldn't know."

Leah said, "Do you and Richard still love each other?"

Myrna said, "What a question!"

Leah said, "Do you?"

Myrna said, "He would trade me for Michelle Pfeiffer. I would trade him for Tom Hanks. Otherwise everything's fine."

Leah said, "You would trade him for Tom Hanks?"

Myrna said, "Maybe not, maybe I should hold out for Gregory Peck."

Leah said, "Gregory Peck died of AIDS."

"No," said Myrna, "that was Rock Hudson."

So it snowed. The snow had trouble sticking in the salt air near the beach but it fell down thick anyway. The fire blazed. The snow kept coming. The wind blew fierce. The willow tree in the garden bent down close to the ground, scratching its branches against the scrubby pale grass. The darkness was broken by the streetlight under whose bulb the white crystals swooped down, rose up in the draft, and disappeared in the hedges beneath. The sea at high tide pushed up the beach almost to the edge of the dunes, black waves pounded. The sand above the water line was smooth, smoothed by the wind. The birds were gone inland. Tucking their heads down under their wings, they waited.

Leah and Ollie and Sally had played three games of Candyland. The dice rolled, the figures moved on the board. Sally smiled. She was visiting Leah. She had explored the house. She had seen the doll's house in Leah's room. She had looked into each of the windows. She lay down on Leah's parents' bed, a large bed with an old quilt of many flowers intertwined. She had taken a nap. Leah had covered her with a blanket. Her large form resting there had looked beached, blown from far away. The bedroom was dusty and there were cobwebs under the chest, in the corners. Leah did not spend time there.

Leah sat next to Ollie on the couch. They were quiet. They watched the fire. They listened to the wind. Ollie said, "Sally needs more sleep than most people. It's part of it. When she gets tired she can't control herself so well."

Leah said, "All of us."

Ollie said, "My mother was patient, so patient. She would play with Sally for hours without stopping. I can't do that."

Leah said, "You do enough."

Ollie said, "There's always more that could be done." He leaned his head back and closed his eyes.

Leah said, "Was it a genetic defect?"

Ollie said, "No."

Leah said, "You understand what I mean?" Then she blushed. "English-major types, my friend Myrna, sometimes don't know about genes, and mutations. They think of everything in moral terms, politics, feelings. I thought you might not know. I'm sorry." Leah got up and took their coffee cups into the kitchen. She came back.

Ollie said, "I know about genes. I believe in evolution. You are a highly evolved woman, large brain size, good hips." Leah laughed. Ollie patted her arm. She sat down and leaned into him. "Tell me about double helixes," he said.

"You don't want to know," she said.

"I do," he said. "If it interests you. I want to know."

She drew him a picture. She tried to be clear. He looked puzzled. "Do you understand?" she asked.

"Enough," he said.

"You're a scientific moron," she said.

"Take your clothes off for me," he said.

Leah said, "Sally is here."

Ollie said, "She'll be asleep awhile. We'll hear her when she wakes."

Leah said, "Maybe we should listen to the weather report. Maybe this is a big storm. Maybe the snow will stick to the ground." She stood up to turn on her radio.

Ollie said, "We don't need the weather report."

Leah said, "But we don't know what it's going to be like tomorrow. We don't know what's coming from Canada or Pennsylvania."

Ollie said, "We'll find out." He stretched his body out, he put his arms up over his head. "It's fine here," he said. "The snow won't stick, it almost never does here. Take your clothes off for me very slowly."

Leah said, "But you've already seen me a lot."

Ollie said, "Please." He said it casually. He said it with a cock of his head toward her. His request was not as trivial as it seemed. He wanted her to do it. Was it because he had asked for something? His mind was concentrated on willing her to pull her sweater over her head, to let her flesh get goose bumps in the air. Leah looked at him carefully. She was not proud of her body. It was not young. Her breasts were not high and firm. Her hips were too wide. She was long, too long, she had hunched her shoulders up over her microscope. She thought her spine might have an unattractive slope at the base of her neck. She had a scar. He had seen it, of course, but now she felt shame.

Ollie said, "I want to see you, to memorize you. I want to see you now." Leah stared at him. This was a new experience. Was he mocking? She thought not. Was she being prudish, stiff, virginal when there was no virginity? Maybe. She decided to do it. She turned her back on him. She lifted up her arms and pulled her old wine sweater off. She held it in her hands and then let it drop to the floor. She took off her T-shirt that said "Bar Harbor Labs" in white letters. She felt the air on her skin. The fire was dying down. It was cold in the room. Outside the window the snow still fell, hitting the side of the house like a mute sighing. Would it still be snowing tomorrow? She turned toward him, her breasts now free. She resisted the impulse to throw her arms across her chest. He was lying there on the cushions staring at her. Leah said, "I'm not pretty. I never have been. My body is too large, my breasts are not even." As she spoke her nipples turned deeper red and rose forward. She could feel them drawing upward as if invisible strings were pulling.

"Go on," said Ollie.

Leah took off her jeans. The slope of her hips turned away from him. "I'm too heavy," said Leah. "I should lose weight."

"No," said Ollie. "Everything is right. Exactly right."

"Of course, you would have to say that," said Leah.

"No," said Ollie as Leah slipped off her red woolen socks and stood before him without any clothes at all. "You are what I want, this way, now." He looked. She stood there. He took off his glasses and rubbed them clean on his flannel shirt. He put them back on. He looked. She saw no recoil, no distaste, nothing distant on his face. "Now you look at me," he said. He stood up and took off his clothes. The fire flickered. The hair on his chest had turned gray. His legs were short and his body, unhelped by weights or jogging, seemed to be round in the belly and there was an extra fold of flesh above his navel. Still he was fine or so Leah thought, not fine exactly but right, just right. After a few silent moments they moved toward each other. They were lying together when Sally woke, thumped hard on the floor as she moved toward the stairs. They hurried and reached for their clothes, which were tumbled together about the couch.

They were not fast enough. Sally saw them. She stood on the third step from the bottom and her hands flew up to her face and down again in a repetitive pattern, like a Charlie Chaplin version of a worker on an assembly line. "Leah," she said, "put on your clothes." Her voice wavered between a question and an order.

Leah said, "I am, Sally. I am."

Ollie said, "We were just going to have hot chocolate. Do you want some?" He was smoothing down his hair, buttoning his shirt, groping for his glasses. Why did she wake now?

Sally stood there. Leah turned on the television. Sally

turned to watch. She turned up the volume. Her large back loomed in front of the screen. The announcer's voice spoke of a heavy snowfall expected by morning in Connecticut.

Leah said, "The illustrations finished?"

Myrna said, "Not yet. The miserable little girl looks like a toad. Her eyes bulge out."

Leah said, "Hyperthyroid?"

Myrna said, "Leave it."

Leah said, "Is Danny still grieving about his snake?"

Myrna said, "He's got stomach problems."

Leah said, "Probably just nerves."

Myrna said, "Or Drano."

Leah said, "You serious?"

Myrna said, "Nah, but the bathroom still stinks."

Leah said, "Does it smell like rotten eggs?"

Myrna said, "Much worse."

Leah said, "Something dead?"

Myrna said, "Very."

Leah said, "How's Sheila?"

Myrna said, "My pearl earrings are gone."

Ollie said to his class, "Who is innocent in this book?"

Bruce Holloway said, "Big deal, she slept with the minister."

Ollie said, "Should she have been punished?"

Ellen said, "They should have punished him, not her."

Ollie said, "He did it alone?"

Mary Harden said, "Sometimes people love each other, and you do things you shouldn't." She blushed.

Ollie said, "There are no consequences? You don't pay for your acts?"

Ellen said, "It was cruel, the letter *A* was cruel."

Ollie said, "Cruel, let's talk about cruel."

In the hall Mary Harden passed by Ollie. Barely stopping, she said, "I need to talk to you alone." This was the first one of the year.

"What do they teach in sex ed?" said Leah.

"The truth," said Ollie, "doesn't always set you free."

While Sally was watching a Mary Poppins video Ollie had brought, they sat together in the kitchen. "So let's talk about something sad," said Ollie.

"Why?" said Leah.

"Because," said Ollie, "the best parts are always sad. I want to know what makes you sad. Tell me."

Leah said, "Nothing. Everything is all right."

Ollie said, "Tell me how your mother died."

Leah said, "She drifted off."

Ollie said, "Like Hamlet's ghost?"

Leah said, "No, like a person who hoards pills."

Ollie said, "You seem so sturdy. Is that an illusion?"

Leah said, "No."

Ollie said, "What happened to your father?"

Leah said, "That makes me cry."

Ollie said, "It's all right. You can cry."

Leah said, "Parkinson's."

Ollie said, "You miss him."

Leah said, "I told you I would cry."

Ollie and Leah sat at the kitchen table in silence. Leah's nose had turned red. Her eyes were puffed. The hum of the TV surrounded them. Leah said, "What's the best thing that ever happened to you?"

Ollie said, "When you came down the beach and helped me pull Sally out of the water."

Leah said, "No, really."

Ollie said, "Really."

When it was time to leave, Leah tried to tie Sally's parka strings. Sally kept pushing her hands away. Leah's fingers brushed against Sally's mouth. Sally opened wide and clamped her teeth down hard. Leah pulled her hand back in time. They said good night at the door. Sally did not look back at Leah. She held her brother's hand tightly as they walked on the wet and icy gravel toward their truck. The waves crashed close enough to hear. The snow had stopped. The air was clear. As they moved away, Leah could see a white mist rising from their mouths. Leah might have called out, "I don't want you to go." Instead she slammed the door firmly against the night and turned out all the lights. When Ollie turned his head the house was in darkness.

Leah went to bed and lay in the dark, the sounds of branches beating against the house. She walked into her parents' bedroom. She straightened the covers. She stood there like a child waiting for someone to take her hand, waiting for the adults to wake.

Myrna said, "I think we're going to get a puppy."

Leah said, "What about Sheila, what will she do to a puppy?"

Myrna said, "Don't say it."

Leah said, "What did Richard give you for your birthday?"

Myrna said, "A gold bracelet. I wear it all the time, except in the shower."

"I'm happy," said Leah.

"Your bathroom?" said Myrna.

"Smells fine," said Leah.

*   *   *

The school Christmas assembly was over. Good King Wenceslas went out on the feast of Stephen. There was a reek in the front hall of hilarity, of tension, of pushing and shoving, and anticipation of pleasure lit up faces, forced them to light up, even if they were afraid, even if they were alone, like some of the kids who wandered like ghosts at a party through the rapidly emptying corridors. Some girls wore red ribbons with little silver bells. They were the senior chorus soprano section.

Sally was waiting for Ollie. He had gone back to his classroom to collect his last papers, the ones that were due the day before the start of vacation. Sally saw a girl with a red ribbon and a silver bell on her sweater. She walked over to the girl. "I want it," she said, pointing to the pin. The girl was startled. She knew Sally. Everyone at school knew Sally. Sally was large and the girl was tiny, her wrists were fragile. She wore bright red lipstick that was not so much sexual as cheerful. She had tied her hair back with a green velvet bow.

The girl said, "It's my pin for being in chorus. Otherwise I'd give it to you."

Sally said, "Give it to me." She knew she was not being nice. She knew she was not being good. She knew Ollie would stop her if he came back right then. She was in a hurry. She put her hand on the girl's sweater and pulled at the pin.

"Don't," shrieked the girl. Sally loomed above her. She did not let go. She pulled hard. The girl had tears in her eyes. It wasn't the pin. It was being pushed and frightened. Sally was a kind of monster, a kind of Freddy, or Halloween creature that marched through the night of horror movies. "You can have it," she said. "Stop pulling."

Sally didn't stop. The girl had everything. She was the same as the others. There was nothing wrong with her.

Ollie came down the hall. He took Sally's arm. He spoke to her very quietly. "Let me help you," he said. "I'm here," he said. "Don't worry," he said, both to Sally and the girl.

"She wants my pin," said the girl to Ollie. "She can have it," she said. "I don't want it anymore." She took it off and Sally reached out her hand. She enclosed the red ribbon and the silver bells in her fist.

"You don't have to do that," said Ollie to the girl.

"It's all right, Mr. Marcus," said the girl. "Have a good vacation, Merry Christmas," she called as she walked quickly away, smoothing her sweater, trailing her book bag.

When Sally opened her fist the red ribbon was crumpled. The tiny pinecone was chipped. The pin was bent. Ollie pinned it on her blouse for her. She patted his hand.

In the car Ollie said to Sally, "Don't ever touch a student, don't ever push a student. Don't even talk to them. Don't go near them. Ever again. I won't bring you to school. I can't trust you to behave yourself." His voice was quiet but there was a tremor in it, a rumble of conviction and betrayal, a hint of hopelessness, exhaustion, and Sally heard it all.

"Yeah, yeah," she said and her tongue thrust forward as it sometimes did without her knowing. This time she knew.

For Hanukkah, Ollie gave Leah a notebook with leaves in blue printed on the cover. Inside it was blank. For your thoughts, he said. She carried it with her in her bag wherever she went. She carried it upstairs and downstairs all through the day. She hadn't written in it yet. When she ran her fingers over the blank pages she felt Ollie near, Ollie looking over her shoulder, Ollie touching her clavicle. Ollie sliding his hand down the top of her shirt and holding her elbow, steering her forcefully into his pickup truck. Ollie driving away with her. Leaving his sister behind.

Leah gave Ollie a copy of *Vogue*, 1946. It had one of her

mother's designs on a model with a veil and dark red lipstick.

"Did your mother look like that?" said Ollie.

"No," said Leah, "that was a model."

Leah gave Ollie a first edition of *Uncle Tom's Cabin*. She
bought it at the library sale.

"This is valuable," he said.

"Not really," said Leah. "There are pages missing." Ollie
placed it on his desk at school where he could look at it
whenever he wanted.

Leah bought an ant farm for Sally. She set it up in the
kitchen. Through a glass window you could watch the ants
move up and down, carrying food, through the levels of
sand. Sally watched it a long time.

Ollie remembered: he had been quiet. He had been a boy
who never spoke in class. He never went up to anyone in
the grassy area near the tire swings and the old jungle gym
that the school board promised to replace but never did. He
kept to himself. He read all the time. He was like a shadow
that receded as you came close. His mother said to him:
"You can invite a friend home after school." He didn't answer her. She held him by the shoulders. She forced his face
up close to hers. "There's nothing to be ashamed of in this
house." He smelled his mother's sweat. She had been lifting
boxes of light bulbs and putting them up on a back shelf. He
spent his time in the cellar. There he had his magazines: old
comics, copies of *Life, Fortune, Newsweek*. He had a collection of paperback books, detective stories. He had his library book of the week. He sat on the stool that had once
belonged to his father's workbench. His father never came
down to the cellar anymore.

Ollie was sick. He had a fever. His mother came to his

side. She felt his forehead. She brought him orange juice. "My ear hurts," he said. She looked at him sadly. Sally was downstairs waiting to be changed. Her husband was in the store. "You'll be all right," she said. The throbbing in his ear got worse. If he shifted his head, a sharp pain went right down into his neck. He was dry and cold at the same time. He counted up to a hundred fifty and back again. He took deep breaths. He banged his hand against the wall. He bit his tongue. He wanted the pain somewhere else in his body, out of his ear. He felt a bubble in his ear. He felt it break and pain came. Then another bubble. He tried to lie still, not to blink an eye, to let the pain pass over him, not find him there. It found him. He was thirsty. His lips were cracked. When he was awake he wanted to sleep. When he was asleep he had bad dreams.

Later his mother came back. "Does your ear still hurt?" she said. "I'm all right," he said. "It's better," he said. He got hot and took off his pajamas. He stayed in his room. He kept his hand over his ear. The pressure of his palm against his skull helped. The pain washed over him. In the morning his father found him white and shaking at the foot of the stairs, wrapped in a blanket. He was talking about ships at sea sinking in storms, about men falling out of the ships, off their decks, into the churning waters. "Get them a lifeboat," he screamed at his father. "Save them," he sobbed. "It's not my fault," he screamed. "I didn't do it. The storm did it."

"Don't let it happen," he begged his father again and again. "I didn't do it," he repeated all the way to the doctor's office. The nurse bathed him in cold water with alcohol. The doctor put drops in his ear.

Once his father came to the top of the cellar steps and called down. "Hey, Ollie," he said, "what're ya doing?"

"Nothing," said Ollie.

"You wanna ride with me?" said his father, who was delivering something to one of the big houses on Water Road. Ollie sat in the cab of the truck next to his father. His father punched him in the arm in a friendly way. Ollie smiled. The smile was shy and quick, almost as if it were unintended, unexpected, an alien pleasure visiting from another world. "Whaddaya say?" Ollie's father asked. Ollie was still. His mouth was closed. "You wanna listen to the baseball game?" His father turned on the radio. Ollie listened.

One winter his father bought him ice skates, black and shiny with a sharp silver blade that flashed in the sun like a knife. He went with his friends to the pond by the cemetery and they played ice hockey, they raced in circles. They pushed each other down and jumped over branches they pulled onto the ice. Ollie was a fast skater, strong and fearless. He would stay on the ice till his nose was bright red and his fingers numb under his gloves. Sometimes on Saturday mornings he would get to the pond so early that he had it all to himself. Then he would skate around the edges like a single bird in flight. He would lie down and look up at the sky. He would pretend he was floating in the pond, staring up through the thick layer of frozen water at the bare willows that bordered the stark gravestones. When the pond was completely frozen and there were no thin dangerous patches, he would take Sally with him. She would watch him from the shore. She would wave her mittened hands in front of her face, back and forth like windshield wipers. She would walk out on the ice after him, slipping and falling, crawling finally, till she found his legs, and she would pull him down. She would rub his face with ice chips. He would hold her hands behind her back. She would punch at his legs. "Hey, Marcus," some boy would call, "get your sister off the ice." He would have to take off his skates and lead her home.

He told Leah, "I was shy for a long time. I was a kind of loner. I ate by myself. I was a peculiar child."

Leah said, "You're not peculiar now."

Ollie sighed. "I'm still peculiar, it's just that everybody else became peculiar too." Fair enough, thought Leah.

André and Litzie had invited Leah over for a drink.

Leah said, "I'm ambitious. I want my name in *Science* or the *New England Journal of Medicine*. I have fantasies of major prizes. I am not resigned to being ordinary."

Litzie said, "Nobody is."

André said, "I'm certainly not."

Leah said, "A cold front is headed this way."

André said, "I don't give a damn about the weather." Leah looked shocked. André said, "I wonder why they don't serve whale in Japanese restaurants. They eat everything else that swims."

Litzie said, "You're boring Leah."

André said, "I am not."

Leah said, "Excuse me," and left the room.

When Leah returned she asked, "Do you consider psychoanalysis a science?"

André said, "I wonder what the id would look like under the microscope. Maybe a black worm with eyes dripping pus and a mouth spitting blood."

Litzie said, "You're a moralist. I see it as a butterfly with white eyes that reflect like mirrors."

Leah said, "The id is a metaphor. Metaphors do not appear under microscopes."

"Depends on your microscope," said André. "God, I'd like to catch a whale, just one, once."

Darkness came early. The deep black hood of the sky covered the beach and the houses of West Pine. The cold and the long nights made everyone hurry home, sleep early, drink more, think of the hard earth in the cemetery and the hard earth of the ball field over by the school and the hard earth of the farms north of the railroad tracks where the corn was plowed down into a flat bed of dried yellow stalks. The train whistled into the blackness. The gates of the crossing closed with their empty tinkle, like the sound of a baby's well-used rattle. No one was riding the evening train but the engineer and the conductor. The empty cars waited a moment in the station and moved on. It was the time of year when in other centuries men and women wrote letters to distant relatives describing their plum cakes, their new clothes, the church sermons. Women whose husbands had gone to sea thought of the other side of the globe, where the sun would still be blistering down and the boats would be rounding horns or capes or coasts with foreign names. Now everyone turned on the television.

Main Street was lit for Christmas with tiny bulbs on evergreens placed in front of each store. In the dark the street shimmered and glowed. Red and green lights, red bows, decorated a large tree at the entrance to the Roman Catholic Church. A crèche with a kneeling Mary and the Three Wise Men and two camels nestled in the grass by the church sign, lettered in white lights, Our Lady of the Perpetual Sea. The Methodist Church had a single candle burning in each window. The street was nearly empty. The stores were closed when Ollie and Leah and Sally went for a walk, the three of them bundled up in mufflers and leather gloves and heavy fuzzy boots. Sally held Leah's hand. She squeezed it tightly.

"Not so tight, Sally," Leah said.

Sally said, "Swing me." She wanted Leah and Ollie to hold her hands and swing her between them. She was too large.

Ollie said, "We can't. You are too big now." She had been too big for many years. She had not asked him to swing her for a long time. Sally smiled.

Leah said, "Grown-up women don't swing."

"Oh," said Sally.

Later Leah and Ollie talked by the light of the television. Sally watched an old movie. Leah said to Ollie, "Were you a brave child?"

Ollie said, "Why?"

Leah said, "You seem like a brave man." Ollie looked down into his coffee cup.

Ollie said, "I was a cowardly child. I was afraid of almost everything. But I learned to hide it."

Leah said, "I wasn't afraid of anything. My father was always saying, Don't do this or that, and I was always saying, I can, I will, Look how high, Look at me with one leg, Look what I can do."

Ollie said, "I believe that."

Leah said, "But then when I grew up I didn't climb the Himalayas or anything like that. I look in microscopes." She was quiet. Perhaps she was thankful she had not been eaten by a lion on some distant snowy peak.

Ollie said, "I was afraid of bats. I saw one in the back of the store, over the shelf that held the boxes of screws. After that I expected them to fly at me from inside closet doors, cupboards, while I was walking to school. I thought they hung in the trees above my head."

"God," said Leah.

"I was afraid of leaves."

"Of leaves."

"I thought they would fall on my head and smother me. In the fall I didn't want to go outside."

"Anything else?" said Leah.

"I was afraid of the ocean. I thought we might have a tidal wave and it would come over our house and drown us," Ollie said.

"What did you do when you were afraid?" asked Leah.

"I went in the cellar," said Ollie.

"You felt safe in the cellar?" said Leah.

"It was all right," said Ollie.

Leah stretched out her hand and touched Ollie's cheek. She ran her fingers over his chin and traced his lips with her thumb. Leah said, "I wish I had known you."

"I'm not afraid now," he said.

"Not even in your dreams?" asked Leah.

"Sometimes in my dreams," said Ollie.

Ollie and Leah went to the movies. Some of his students were ahead of him on line. They saw him with a woman. There was head turning and whispering. Leah was embarrassed. She moved out from under his arm. "No," said Ollie. "I want everyone to see I'm with you." Leah longed for the line to move. It didn't. It was cold on the street and she could feel her nose turning red and leaking. She wiped it with her glove, leaving a stain on the leather. This embarrassed her too. She pulled away.

Ollie said, "What's the matter, are you ashamed of being with me?" Leah felt her stomach lurch.

"Why would I be ashamed?" she asked.

"Big-city scientist, doctorate, rich lady with a summer home, with me, small-town schoolteacher, local college. I understand the pecking order of things. I'm not a prize in your circles," Ollie answered.

Leah hesitated. It was true that he was from a different place. It was true that long ago back in college she had thought of herself, if she thought of herself with someone, with a Nobel laureate, a professor of international reputation, an inventor of a new technology, a discoverer of asteroids or acids in action.

"I have no circles," she said. She paused to consider. "No, that's not right, tonight you are my circle." Ollie put his arm back around her. Leah stared straight ahead. The line moved forward. Leah's toes seemed stuck together in her boots. She felt as if everyone were looking at her. They weren't. Even the high school students had turned back to each other. Leah put her hand on Ollie's shoulder as they walked through the door. She thought he might lose her in the crowd surging toward the ticket booth. She did not want to be lost.

"The cold front will bring rain tomorrow," she said.

"I'll remember to take my umbrella," Ollie said, pinching her right through her coat.

They sat in the back row. Ollie preferred not to get too close to the screen. He needed some distance, especially in violent movies where the blood spilled. He would flinch and duck and press his spine against the back of the chair. If he sat up front he got dizzy. In the theater when the lights went out Ollie put his arm around Leah and pulled her as near to him as he could. He rubbed her wrist with his hand. He circled it with his broad fingers. He leaned into her side. He put his hand on her breast and pressed in. He fondled her hair. He pulled at her ear. She had trouble following the plot of the movie. "Later," she said, but he couldn't wait.

"Leah," he said, "I have a plan for the rest of our lives."

Leah said nothing. Did he mean it?

Myrna said, "He has a retarded sister that comes with the deal."

Leah said, "We have no deal."

Myrna said, "Maybe he'll send her away."

Leah said, "I don't think so. I wouldn't ask."

Myrna said, "Why not?"

Leah said, "They're very close. He's all she has."

Myrna said, "Are you his sister's keeper?"

Leah said, "I don't mind."

Myrna said, "Not yet, you don't."

Leah said, "I'm overexcited. I get nervous tremors in my stomach. I feel like I'm about to perform all the time. When I was going to Paris to work at the Pasteur I had this too."

Myrna said, "Love."

Leah said, "Fear."

Myrna said, "Has he asked you to move in with him?"

Leah said, "No."

Myrna said, "Be careful. There's a reason he's available."

Boris said, "I'm buying a secondhand Honda, thirty thousand miles, that's all."

Leah said, "Why don't you get a pickup truck?"

Boris said, "What would I do with a pickup truck?"

Leah said, "I like them, that's all."

Boris said, "This teacher, he drives one?"
Leah said, "Dodge, 1984."

Sally lay in her bed and looked out her small window. She
saw over the eaves of the roof, past the small pipe used to
vent the kitchen and into the trees that bordered the road.
She stared at the moon. It was swollen and white. It seemed
to hang close to the earth. She put her fingers in her mouth
and nibbled gently at her thumb. She rocked herself back
and forth, listening to the familiar scrape of the bed against
the floor. She put her hands on her breasts, heavy breasts.
They had grown large years ago. Her mother had said they
were good. She had known they were good. She was almost
asleep. She could feel sleep flowing toward her and ebbing
away. She could feel dreams rising, shapes and faces, a train
track, an old doll, the skirt of a dress, Mrs. Roomey's neck
with her purple beads strung sloping down her chest. But
the dream didn't stay, it slipped away and turned to darkness, to waiting, to thoughts that were not exactly thoughts.
Her big body thumped from side to side as if sleep were
waiting on the left or the right. Her pillow had fallen to the
floor. She banged her head lightly against the wall. Sweet
Sally, her mother would say, tomorrow we will crayon, tomorrow we will make chocolate pudding, tomorrow we will
go to the store and I will make you a dress. Sweet Sally,
sweet dreams. Sally remembered.

Ollie was asleep in the next room. She stood up and went
to the hall. She walked down toward his room. She rubbed
her eyes, which seemed to still want to be closed. She
pushed at his door, half-open. She saw him sleeping, his
plaid flannel pajamas were visible in the moonlight. His
attendance book was on the floor. His glasses lay on the

newspaper that was crumpled on his chair. He was a big man sleeping in a boy's room. His feet stuck out from under the covers at the end of the bed. His feet were white and so clean they looked like he had never stepped anywhere, not on the wooden floor, not in the yard. Sally bent down to look at the hairs that grew from his toes. She looked at the bones in his ankle, a knobby one sticking out. She wanted to put her fingers on it but she didn't.

She stood there watching him. He turned over on his stomach, burrowing his head down into his sheets. He turned back onto his side. His gray hair curled across his pillow. Sally came closer. She wanted to touch his arm but she knew she shouldn't wake him. He had explained it carefully. He needed to work, to go to school, and he had to sleep. She could watch television in the living room. She could stay in her room. She could sit in the chair in his room quietly but she could not wake him. Sometimes she did anyway. Tonight she just watched him. She wanted to stroke his face with her hand. She wanted to lie down on the bed next to him but there was no room. She knelt down on the floor and put her face close up to his. She could feel his breath coming in and out.

She had trouble doing things gently, sometimes she rushed her gestures, sometimes she pulled hard when she meant just to brush something. That was why cups broke and why Mrs. Roomey served her lunch on a paper plate. "Don't be rough," Ollie would say. She would imagine herself picking something up, pulling a towel off the rack with just the right amount of force, but sometimes she was too sudden, too hard, or nothing happened. She had not pulled hard enough or held on tight enough, and something slipped or didn't move or turned over. Some days she could put the red buttons on the numbers on the bingo card and some days she would miss. Now she concentrated as hard as she could. Now she made her mind think about her muscles and what they should do and she bent her face forward and with her lips, just the right amount, just like a feather falling to the ground, she kissed Ollie. He moved in his sleep. He did not wake. She was pleased. She did it again, just right, a moist opening of lips just where he would shave in the morning. She stayed on the floor by his side till she felt her body get heavy. Then she got up and walked back into her room. The moon had moved higher in the sky and she could no longer see it when she lay down. That was all right. She closed her eyes and sleep came and stayed.

New Year's Eve. Ollie's colleague Henry Morton and his wife, Hilda, were having a party. Every New Year's Eve for the past eighteen years, the Mortons had had a party. Ollie and Sally went every year. At the party Sally would blow noisemakers. She would eat plates and plates of food. Toward midnight when the music turned slower and someone sang Auld Lang Syne, Ollie would take Sally onto the floor where the carpet had been rolled back for the evening, and with his arm around her waist he would rock her back and forth. He didn't lead, he didn't do anything fancy. He just held her and she would press close to him. Soon after midnight he would take her home. This New Year's Eve, Leah came with Ollie and Sally. Her long hair was held back with a gold clip. She had put on a green silk blouse she had found in her mother's closet. She wore high heels and black stockings. She had bought makeup at the drugstore and her face was paler than usual but her eyelashes were dark. Her eyes were mysterious, dark, sad, a little smudged.

Ollie said, "I shouldn't be taking you to the Mortons'. I

should be taking you to the Rainbow Room and we should be dancing under the colored lights. We should be in Paris." For the first time in his life he yearned to be in Paris.

"Why?" said Leah.

"It would suit you more."

"I don't think so," said Leah. Ollie knew that passion was not a bottomless well. Life would cap it. Nevertheless Leah in her green blouse and her dark eye makeup and the shine of the material in her skirt and the tilt of her head brought him bittersweet dread, dread of dying young, a heart attack, a malignancy, a stroke, a car accident, a fire. Please, God, he wanted a long life. He must have a long life. Heat spread across his face. He wished that he knew how to waltz. He would waltz with Leah in the Mortons' living room. "Happy New Year," he whispered in her ear.

Leah talked to the biology teacher. They discussed frogs. Leah explained the advantage of mice for experimental purposes. The biology teacher hung on each of Leah's words, often repeating them so he wouldn't lose them in the fog of wine that was drifting across his right and left brain.

It was their first public appearance. Ollie said, "We met on the beach."

Leah said, "I'm spending the winter."

Ollie said, "She's a scientist with Rockefeller. Taking some time off."

Leah said, "My mother planted an herb garden each spring."

Ollie said, "Her parents came from Europe."

Leah said, "I bicycle a lot. I go for walks."

Ollie said, "I took her out to the state park."

Leah said, "Yes, it's quieter in the winter. I like it better."

Just before midnight, when the Mortons turned out the lights and let the candles on their table flicker and the music got slower and slower, Sally came over to Leah. "Dance," she said. Leah had a moment of fright. She looked to find Ollie. Rescue me, she thought. He was out of sight. She put her arms out to Sally, and Sally grasped Leah by the waist. She pulled her close and held her tight. They moved together to the music. Leah felt Sally's breasts pushing against hers. Sally was the larger woman. She was heavier. She stepped on Leah's feet. Leah tried to move her legs so they would avoid Sally's feet. She smelled the chocolate chip cookies that Sally had been eating, the Fritos and the popcorn and the onion dip. Leah said to Sally, "Happy New Year."

Sally said, "Happy New Year."

Leah said, "I think it will be."

Sally said, "Are you my best friend?"

Leah said, "I'm too old to have a best friend."

Leah had a few glasses of wine and a cup of brandy punch. She felt the room spin. The music was loud in the den. She took off her shoes. She began to dance. She had no partner. She just moved as if no one else were in the room. It cleared her head. She thumped on the floor. She waved her arms frantically to a beat of blood cascading down hidden rocks in a far-off jungle. It was good for her double helixes to get shaken around. It was good for her DNA and RNA and her spleen and her liver and her tissue and her marrow to bounce in the night. Ollie moved toward her. He tried to dance too. He tried hard. His body moved shyly, awkwardly, clumsily offbeat, up and down. "I can't," he said. Leah went on without him.

Later Ollie drifted over to the food table. The crackers were almost all gone. The remains of the guacamole dip had turned brown, there was a wine stain on the cloth. The candles had burned down, only a small flame remained. Ollie felt glad, gladness came over him, followed by alarm. He put his hand out over the flame. He let the glow warm his wrist for a moment and then he pressed down. He said nothing. He held his arm and rushed to the kitchen for ice. "I burned myself," he said to his hostess. "My hand slipped." The pain continued. He let it come, wave after wave. Leah helped Hilda Morton wrap his hand in ointment and gauze.

André came to Leah's house one Saturday morning. He shifted from foot to foot, cold air rushing into her kitchen till she invited him in. She was having tea and looking at printouts of data gathered a few years back.

André said to Leah, "My wife is worried my brain is going."

Leah said, "Stop talking about whales."

André said, "Why is it so hard to get someone to believe me?"

Leah said, "Would you like an alfalfa sprout and tomato sandwich?"

André said, "Do you have mustard?"

Leah said, "I think I'm losing my mind too."

André said, "I thought you were fond of this man."

Leah said, "I am. More than fond. He's making me sick. I got socked, bam, pow, knocked out. I don't like it."

André said, "Give it up."

Leah said, "I can't."

André said, "You protected yourself too long."

Leah said, "Why?"

André said, "You tell me."

Leah said, "Does it matter?"

André said, "Not now."

Leah said, "Do you think there's something wrong with Ollie?"

André said, "Of course."

Leah said, "I'm serious."

André said, "Me too. Now let's talk about Pinocchio. Remember, he was swallowed by a whale."

Leah said, "Please."

Later that night André was lying in bed next to Litzie. She was wearing an old sweatshirt for warmth. Her gray hair was wet from her shower. Her skin was pale and there were folds under her neck. She leaned against André's arm and petted him while absently reading her book, a biography of Melanie Klein. He put his hand over the page. She looked up, her reading glasses falling forward.

"Listen," he said, "whale blubber was once more valuable — "

Litzie said, "When will you let it be."

André said, "It was real. I was swallowed by a whale."

Litzie said, "Go to sleep."

André said, "Maybe I was swallowed by the whale because you've lost your love for me."

Litzie said, "That must be it."

André said, "Will Leah be able to love Ollie? Will Ollie be able to love Leah?"

Litzie said, "In a book, yes. In reality, no."

André said, "You're wrong."

Litzie said, "They waited too long. They're scared. They're not brave enough."

André said, "They are."

Ollie remembered the day he had gone with his parents to take Sally to see the specialist in New York. The store was dark. There was a sign in the window, Closed for Family Business. His grandfather in Brooklyn had talked about what you said to God to keep yourself in God's mind, to keep God in your mind. Every morning, every evening, prayers. But his grandfather spoke to God in song, or almost song. Ollie did not know the tune. He couldn't remember it. God, what did God speak? God had no special embrace for Ollie, of this the boy was sure. But he did hope. Didn't his mother say specialists knew things that other doctors didn't, that this specialist was recommended by a customer who was a doctor, an ear, nose, and throat doctor? The doctor had said his colleague was a genius. A genius is a person who can do things others have given up on, a genius is a person who defies the ordinary. Ollie did not believe in miracles but he did believe in genius. The ear, nose, and throat doctor had come to the store to buy chicken wire to make a fence on his property to keep the deer away from his wife's vegetable garden. He had seen Sally sitting on the countertop. He had suggested a visit. He had arranged the appointment. Ollie's mother had saved for five months in a special box for the money for the city doctor. Ollie's father had said it wouldn't matter, they shouldn't go, but Ollie's mother had said they must. She had said she would never sleep again if they didn't. She had complained of headaches and backaches and she had brought it up again and again to her husband until he had said he would take Sally to the city doctor.

The doctor had held Sally on his lap and looked into her eyes with his instrument. He had pulled at her legs and run his fingers down her spine. He had asked her to turn this way or that, to jump up and down. He then placed her in a small chair and his nurse came in and together they attached wires to Sally's scalp. They used Vaseline on little black clips and parted her hair to reach her skin. Sally was frightened when she saw the wires. She was frightened when the nurse came near her. She had liked the doctor, but standing near the machine and its lights blinking, she saw the doctor's double chin, his hairy thumb, his eyes round behind his glasses, and she was frightened. Her mother was right there, Ollie was by her side, holding her hand, telling her it was all right. Her father was waiting in the outside room. He had promised her a treat.

"See the tongue," the doctor said to his nurse. The nurse watched Sally's tongue moving forward and back.

"She can't help it," said her mother.

"What a pretty girl," said the nurse. "Such pretty hair."

Sally moaned. Something terrible was about to happen. Then she felt the prick of the electricity as it flowed through the wires. Her hands flew to her head and she tried to pull off the wires but the nurse was too quick and grabbed her hands. Sally screamed and screamed. Ollie put his hands up over his ears to block the sound. He saw her mouth open.

"Please, please stop it," he begged both the doctor and Sally.

"Don't move," shouted the doctor. They used straps. They used cloth bandages to tie her up.

She stared at Ollie. She kicked her legs until the nurse tied those too.

"Help me," she called out over and over again. Ollie was numb. He felt nothing. He moved like a robot toward his mother. She was staring at Sally. Her dress was stained dark in wide circles under her arms.

Later, in the car going home, Sally's mother had held her on her lap. Her father had said, "I told you."

Her mother said, "We had to try."

Her father said, "You had to try."

Her mother said, "They don't know everything."

Her father said, "I'm tired."

Sally fell asleep with her head against the pane of the window. She made gulping noises when she slept, like a person whose air passages were clogged, like a person who had swallowed something lumpy and spongy and it was stuck in the throat.

"Sweetheart," said Sally's mother to her child and stared straight ahead at the highway.

"We had to close the store all day for this," said Sally's father.

"We'll make it up," said her mother.

When they pulled the car into the driveway they saw Isobel, a neighbor's dog, a small dog with white fur, standing under their beech tree. She barked. Ollie was afraid to get out of the car. He didn't want the dog to see him move. He knew that the dog would bite him. "Stay in the car, then," said his father and slammed the door. Ollie curled up on the backseat and then it was dark and he couldn't see, maybe the dog was still there, maybe it wasn't. Maybe it was hiding behind a bush. Maybe it wasn't. He finally fell asleep. His father found him in the morning, hungry and cold, his back pressed against the seat cushions. The dog was no longer there.

It was very late. The full flat white moon had passed over to the morning side of the sky. Leah lay awake in Ollie's bed. She could hear the television set, an old movie, down in the living room. Sally might have been there watching or sleeping in the chair, the blanket pulled up over her shoulders, the cat on her lap. Leah stretched her legs. Ollie shifted toward her. He held her in his right arm, his left arm pulled across her chest, so she couldn't move too far away. The bed was narrow enough, a shift of her shoulders and she might fall to the floor. She curled herself up against his broad body. He was warm from sleep, warm from her heat. In his sleep his penis stiffened, a thought, a dream, the closeness to her hips. She smiled. She rocked a little. He burrowed his head in her shoulder. She was careful not to lean against his bandaged hand. She wanted to sleep but she did not want to sleep. She wanted to stay awake so she could feel his shape leaning against her, making sure that he was really there, that the smell of his hair and his breath, the outline of his glasses on the table, her own sweater thrown over his chair, this was true and not a wish, that this pressure against her thighs was coming from his body, not her mind, that the moon that seemed to come closer to the small window, to press itself against her eye as it made its way toward its ocean bed, was witness to her happiness, not mocking, but approving. Leah held her body still so he wouldn't be disturbed. She watched the moon.

Leah heard the sound of footsteps up the stairs, down the hall. Sally. Sally not going toward her bedroom but turning toward Ollie's. Leah pulled the blanket up over her shoulders. Ollie shifted with her movement. He held her tightly so that she couldn't easily slide downward. She turned her face into the pillow. Her long dark hair was pinned under Ollie's arm. The door flew open. It banged against the wall. Sally stood in the frame, her heavy form outlined. Leah closed her eyes.

Ollie sat up. "What is it?" he said. Sally stood there. "Go to bed," said Ollie. Sally pulled the covers off. Leah put up her hands, reached for the sheets, cried out all at once. Sally slapped at Leah's bare skin. She pinched her breast.

Ollie jumped up. He shouted at Sally, "No." He pushed her away from the bed. She was bigger than he was. Sally's eyes were narrowed. Her tongue flicked in and out. Her big hands waved. "No," he said again. Sally banged the door closed. They could hear her footsteps on the stairs and then the TV was turned up very loud.

Leah put her hand on Ollie's groin. Her nipples rose in expectation. "Not now," he said. Ollie stared at the ceiling. "I can't hurt her," he said. "You understand?" he asked. Leah nodded.

"That's why you never married?" asked Leah. Ollie said nothing.

Sally sat in the living room. The TV flickered on and on. She picked at her fingernails. Her mother had told her not to do that. Her father had kissed her fingers, each one in turn, "Nice fingers," he said. "Don't hurt them." But it was hard not to tear at the cuticles with her teeth, with her other hand. After he had died, at the funeral, which was in Brooklyn because back then there was no Jewish Center in West Pine, she had picked up her hands and put them in her mouth and bit and bit till the flesh was raw. Her mother had tried to stop her. Ollie had held one of her hands. But she had broken it free and bit some more. Now she went into the kitchen and in a drawer found the scissors that Mrs. Roomey let her cut with. They were broad and thick but good enough. She pulled the bands off her braids and, taking her hair in small pieces, she cut and cut. The dark hairs fell to the floor in front of the TV. Ollie wouldn't be able to braid her hair anymore.

In the dark in her room with the moon in the window she pressed her thighs together, squeezing some moisture onto her body, an excitement rising and falling, going nowhere. Alone, she was alone. Alone she lay down on the bed and her hands felt for her large breasts, which only the doctor touched once a year when Ollie took her to him. The first time it had happened she had screamed. Ollie told her it was all right. He had stayed with her while she was examined. It was all right. Now she put her hands there and pushed back and forth. Alone, she was alone. She knew her mother was gone. She knew her father was gone. Ollie was there but not alone. She broke into a sweat and the sheet turned wet. Alone, she was alone, alone, alone. This was not her word. Her word was Mama, her word was Papa, her word was Ollie. Her word was Sally. She had drawn lines to connect those words. The lines were split, frayed, led nowhere. Alone was not her description, her report to her mind of her mind. It was her experience, wordless, the aloneness was uncontained, offered no end to itself, went on and on through the long night.

Myrna said, "My stepdaughter threatens to move out, to go back to live with her mother. Her therapist said she's conflicted. I'll say she's conflicted."

Leah said, "Does your bathroom still smell?"

Myrna said, "Yes."

Leah said, "Try a heavy-duty alcohol-based solvent with an antimildew acid."

Myrna said, "If I die suddenly, have me tested for Drano."

Leah said, "I'm sorry it's so hard."

Myrna said, "It's hard."

Leah said, "Ollie seems sad. Sometimes he has nothing to say to me. Sometimes we're together and I can feel him drift away."

Myrna said, "Don't worry. Men are like that. The closer you get, the quicker the old walls go up."

Leah said, "Really."

Myrna said, "Really, don't worry."

Leah said, "His nostrils are too wide. He blinks without his glasses. He can never find his car keys. Just because his students follow him around doesn't mean anybody else should."

Myrna said, "Are you saying you're tired of him?"

"No," Leah said. "I think he's going to leave me."

Myrna said, "Any evidence of this defection?"

Leah said, "No, just silences, odd silences."

Myrna said, "Ignore them."

Leah said, "Sometimes I think I'm going to leave him."

Myrna said, "Why? I thought you were happy."

Leah said, "I am."

Myrna said, "I don't understand."

Leah said, "Sometimes I don't want to be happy. I feel invaded. I feel imposed on. I feel burdened. I want to go away by myself."

Myrna said, "You'd better go back to work."

Leah said, "I haven't any ideas. You know I need ideas."

Myrna said, "Get one."

Leah said, "I will, I will soon. Who says everyone has to do something? I don't have to do anything at all."

Myrna said, "Good for you."

Leah said, "You don't believe me?"

Myrna said, "You're a microbiologist, last I heard."

Leah said, "I'm not if I don't want to be."

Myrna said, "What do you think about all day?"

Leah said, "Sex."

Myrna said, "I envy you."

"Really," said Leah, "how nice."

Myrna said, "My gold bracelet, I was in the shower. I came out, it was gone."

Leah had not forsaken science. Ollie was at school. Sally was home with Mrs. Roomey. Leah was in her house listening to a Mozart quartet. Her feet were up on the couch, curled under her. Her head was leaning back against the cushion. She reached her arm forward for her tea, which was in a cup on the table in front of her. Suddenly she thought of the arms of the proteins, receptors pulling toward the cell, the chemicals of choice, needed for reproduction, stimulation, creation of new directions, commanders of new functions. Her hand became the receptor. She saw it move slowly in front of her. The design of an experiment, a method to discover what was in that hand, came to her. She stood up. She felt a shaking in her legs. She repeated the thought. She went to her table and made a drawing. She considered her drawing. She saw that her calf muscle was twitching. It was excitement. She rubbed her leg. She felt hot and cold. She gulped down her tea. She had an idea. The first real idea in a long time. She couldn't sit still. She couldn't think about it any further. She let the waves of excitement well up within her. It was a good feeling. It was the old feeling. She didn't need to pursue it now. It would wait for a calmer moment. It would wait for her attention, but it was there, her idea, sitting in the center of her mind, a treasure, a secret, a throbbing point of glory inside her skull. She drank her tea and listened to the music and realized how long it had been, too long, very long, but it didn't matter because now she had an idea, a new idea of her own. Where had it come from? From her hand reaching for her tea, from the Mozart quartet, from the afternoon haze, from the night before, when she had been leaning against Ollie in bed, from where? It didn't matter. She wrote the first sentences, a formula, a diagram, in the notebook with blue leaves Ollie had given her.

In the parking lot by the main beach the cars huddled together like sheep. The radios were blaring. A crowd of high school kids were watching one car circling and circling around, leaving tire marks on the tar. There were beer bottles on the hoods of the cars. There were headlights focused on the cold beach, where the waves were large and heavy. Ollie drove up with Leah. "Something I have to do," he said. He got out of the Dodge, wrapping the scarf Leah had given him tight around his neck. There was a quieting of the crowd as they spotted him. He moved right into the center of a group of boys.

"What's up?" he said. There was a smell of beer and nicotine, a rutting smell of lipstick and gum, hair spray and the moist cardboard of pizza boxes.

"What are you doing here, Mr. Marcus?" someone called.

"Came to join you," he said. He motioned to Leah to come out of the truck. She came. Embarrassed. It seemed the wrong place to be. "Are you going to offer us something to drink?" he said. There was a shuffling about. "What's the game?" he said. "Are you playing a game?" said Ollie. Ollie saw Bruce Holloway. "Hey, you. I thought you were joining the Marines this spring."

"I am," said Bruce.

"If you get out of high school," said Ollie. He stood there. A girl giggled.

"We were just going, Mr. Marcus," said someone.

"Nothing happened."

"Everything's cool." The cars drifted off, one after another. Ollie and Leah stood alone in the parking lot, their breath white in the winter air.

"Just letting them know I know," said Ollie. "Nobody dares come into their pack in the dark. I dare."

In the dark, in the parking lot, Leah leaned against Ollie's side. "I wish," she said, "I were you."

"No, you don't," he said.

"I mean," she said, "I wished on the first star I saw to-night."

"Have you blown a scientific fuse?" Ollie said.

"I made my wish," she said.

"What was it?" Ollie asked.

Leah turned her head away. "My wish had no words."

Ollie said, "The only kind that come true." He squeezed her hand, he nibbled her ear. In the back of the car, his legs too long, her legs too long, at the beach, like kids, with the radio giving the news, they rubbed each other, they slid on top of each other, tucking limbs here and there, and they sank together into a place of their own making.

"We could," said Ollie. "You could move in with us."

"Sally wouldn't like it," said Leah.

"I miss you in the morning. I want to see you when I come back from school. I want you in my house," said Ollie.

Leah said, "This has never happened to me before."

Ollie said, "You were waiting for me."

Leah said, "I don't believe in love."

Ollie said, "Neither do I."

Leah said, "I mean it."

Ollie said, "I promise no alarming words."

Leah said, "What if this is a bad idea?"

Ollie said, "We'll find out."

Leah said, "I couldn't bear it."

Ollie said, "Neither could I."

He brought her a Valentine nevertheless. It was a red flower on a box of chocolates. He brought Sally a box of chocolates with a card that had a puppy on it, pulling at a little girl's socks.

"I want the flower," said Sally. Ollie looked embarrassed. "I want the flower," Sally shouted. Ollie gave Sally the flower from Leah's box.

"You don't have to give her everything she wants," said Leah.

"You don't understand," said Ollie.

"No, I don't," said Leah, who knew it was ridiculous to make a scene about a paper flower. Sally ate all the chocolates, leaving little gold wrappers all over the floor. Ollie bent to pick them up. Leah refused to help.

Leah said, "He's asked me to move in with him."

Myrna said, "And you're going to?"

Leah said, "I said I'd think about it. I'll never get used to her."

Myrna said, "Try a residential setting, a hospital, an institution, a home with twenty-four-hour care."

Leah said, "He won't."

Myrna said, "What are you going to do?"

Leah said, "Move in with him and with her."

Myrna said, "We're tearing out the pipes. The wall behind the tub has to go too."

Leah said, "What a mess."

Myrna said, "What do you think is in there?"

Leah said, "Something that stinks."

Leah walked around her house. She thought about leaving it. Closing down the heat, turning off the lights. She felt alarmed, distant from herself, as if she were followed by a shadow, a ghost in the room. She sat on her parents' bed. She could take the quilt with her, it was a warm heavy quilt. The wallpaper was still good, roses and vines, a country paper. She liked it. What would she do with her mother's clothes, the ones she'd designed? What was she doing to herself? She stretched tall. She thought she heard a noise. She shivered. I don't want to do this, she thought. I don't like him, she thought, not well enough, I don't, not to move in. I never wanted to move in with anyone, she thought. She did want to. She knew she did, with Ollie. She thought about Sally. Sally would never know the pleasure of algebra. Algebra was one of Leah's greatest pleasures. Sally would never have a friend who didn't pity her. Sally would never have a man put his thumb in her belly button. Sally was ugly. She had ugly habits. Maybe she didn't want to move in with Ollie. Maybe she wanted to go back to the city, to her real life.

Boris said, "You have a new approach?"
    Leah said, "Yes."
    Boris said, "When can we start?"
    Leah said, "I'm not sure."
    Boris said, "Is he treating you right?"
    Leah said, "What a sexist thing to say."
    Boris said, "Are you treating him right?"
    Leah said, "Yes and no."

Leah called Myrna.
    Leah said, "I'm not sure."
    Myrna said, "Maybe I should meet this hero."
    Leah said, "I'm afraid I'm making a mistake."
    Myrna said, "You could move in and then move out."
    Leah said, "I know."
    Myrna said, "Does his bathroom smell?"
    Leah said, "No."
    Myrna said, "Lucky you."

*   *   *

Ollie was in the school lunchroom waiting for Bruce Hollo-way to bring him a late paper. He felt a sinking in his stom-ach. Maybe it was a mistake to ask Leah to move in. How well did he know her? He had never considered that any-thing about his living arrangements would change. His life had balance. He might have dared more than he should, more than he was allowed, maybe he had shifted the ground and triggered an earthquake, a mud slide that would bury him. He had to think of Sally, how hard this would be for her.

Leah was a distraction, a temptation, not reality, not his reality. She would lose interest in him. What did he know about the things she cared about? She would have to go back after a while. She would need to work. She would find him boring. She would find West Pine boring. Where would he be then? Only children think love is enough, take wild chances, throw themselves after their hormones, recklessly. If she knew him, if she knew the man he was, she would never stay. His head ached. He put his fingers up to mas-sage his temples. Bruce Holloway was staring at him, paper in hand.

He came to Leah's house. He sat on her couch. He said very little. His eyes wandered to the Indian print on the wall and out the window at the evergreen shaking in the wind. He had nothing to say.

"Is something wrong?" asked Leah. She sat next to him and put her hand on his thigh. It felt like the trunk of a tree. He didn't turn to her. "What is it?" she said.

"I have moods," he said.

She said, "That's all right." But it wasn't.

They took a drive with Sally to see the lobster boats un-load at the marina. He was quiet in the pickup truck. Leah was on the outside of the seat. Sally spread her legs so that Leah was crushed up against the door handle. Ollie said nothing the entire trip.

"Why aren't you talking?" asked Leah.

"No reason," said Ollie. "We don't have to talk all the time."

But this wasn't just space, rest, this was the digging of a chasm, quiet work, silent steady work, the purchase of a ticket out.

Leah felt that she was in one of those exercises they gave you in college, the self-help, save-yourself, cure-your-madness sessions, lean back against the air, let your partner catch you, let yourself go into someone's arms, don't look, close your eyes, just fall, fall. She could never do it. She would never do it: turn out your own light, get your own towel from the closet, fix your own pancakes, get your own aspirin down from the medicine chest, don't wait up for a hand or a stroke, don't tell anyone your nightmares, they have their own. She had taught herself well, knees stiff, eyes awake, look around, don't fall, not into anyone's promises. That was the glory of her lab, inside her door, by her table, with her tubes and her wires and her splitters and her mice, it was there or it was not, you proved it or you didn't, there was no depending on viewpoint, no shading away from the truth, no falling down expecting one thing and finding another.

She told Ollie she couldn't see him that night. She had work to do. He did not complain.

Ollie called Leah the next day. "I think you shouldn't move in this week. Sally needs time."

Leah said, "You need time?"

Ollie said, "It's not that."

Leah said, "It is that."

Ollie said, "Leah, I can't rush."

Leah said, "I wouldn't want you to rush."

Ollie said, "I have to think."

Leah said, "I have to think too."

Ollie said, "I don't mean I don't want to see you."

Leah said, "What do you mean?"

Ollie said, "I have to take care of Sally."

Leah said, "I see."

Ollie said, "No, you don't."

Leah said, "I'm busy. I'm working."

Ollie said, "I'll call."

Leah said, "Thank you for a good time."

Ollie said, "Don't say that." Leah hung up the phone.

Leah said to Litzie, "I am going back to the city."

Litzie said, "You are no longer attached to Oliver Marcus?"

Leah paused. She said, "He doesn't interest me."

Litzie said, "Now, suddenly?"

Leah said, "I don't think it's going to work out. I don't care."

Litzie said, "You want some tea?"

Leah said, "Really, I don't care."

There was silence between the two women. The older one looked at the clock. The younger one looked at her hands.

Leah said, "He doesn't like me."

"Did he tell you?" said Litzie.

"I just know," said Leah.

"Make him tell you," said Litzie.

Leah said, "Did you hear the weather report tonight?"

Litzie said, "I can't remember what it said, no storm, though, that's something."

Leah said, "What did they say about a cold front, how many more days till it passes, what about the windchill factor?"

Litzie said, "You should talk to Ollie. You shouldn't pull back. Talk to him, find out what he's thinking."

Leah said, "He doesn't want to tell me."

Litzie said, "Men need help. They have trouble with their tongues. They tend to choke when they have something important to say. Help him."

Leah said, "André, does he talk to you?"

"Sometimes," said Litzie. Then she added, "Sometimes too much. Sometimes the wrong things. When he doesn't speak clearly, I hear, what is the name? Those insects that eat wood, eating away at the beams, crunch, crunch, tearing down what we have built."

"You've been married so long," said Leah.

"Don't let him sneak out, hiding behind his face, shrinking his heart so you can't see it. Don't let him be a coward," said Litzie.

Leah said, "I'm a coward too."

Litzie said, "I know."

Ollie talked to his class. "The fish, what was it? What do you think?" A hand went up.

Martha said, "It was Christ."

Ollie said, "What else?"

"Couldn't be Christ," said Bruce. "It didn't resurrect. It just died, took forever about it, but it died."

"I liked *Jaws* better," said Alan, who hardly ever said anything.

"The old man," said Ollie. "You admired him?"

"Yeah, he was great," said Bruce.

"Why?" said Ollie.

"Like Indiana Jones, he wouldn't quit. You could tear off parts of him and he just kept going," said Bruce.

"He should've had a radio and a rifle," said Mark.

"He was an example of the third world person whom we should aid to have a better way of life," said Martha.

"What should we do for him?" asked Ollie.

"Fishing nets, ultrasound radios, life jackets, modern equipment, for God's sake," said Howard.

"Was he brave?" said Ollie. The class nodded. "So what do you think, the battle between man and fish, could it happen to you?"

"It's a boy's book," said Martha. "Any woman would have gone home and opened a can of tuna fish." The girls giggled.

"He lasted a long time, he didn't let the fish go. He was all right," said Bruce.

"Big deal," said Martha. "He didn't bring anything back. In the end he had nothing."

Ollie said, "Were you sad at the end?" The class considered. The bell rang.

Ollie was tired. His limbs ached. "Leah, Leah, Leah Rose," he said to himself. Maybe he was getting a flu. His stomach curled and released. It was one of those days. He slammed the door of his pickup shut. "Asshole," he shouted at no one in particular. He pulled up in front of his house. Mrs. Roomey was out on the front steps waving at him. "What is it?" he called as he quickly lifted himself out of the truck. He had to call Leah. He wanted to see Leah. He needed Leah.

"Sally," she said, "is gone."

"Where?" asked Ollie.

Mrs. Roomey shook her head. Her face was white and she kept brushing her hands through her hair as if smoothing it would return the missing woman.

"How long?" said Ollie.

"I thought she was watching TV. I heard the TV. I was in the kitchen. I was cleaning out the refrigerator. You left the Chinese dinner from last week in the cartons in the back. I couldn't have left her more than half an hour. Maybe a little more. I called her and she didn't answer. I went into the living room and she wasn't there. I looked upstairs. I looked in the bathrooms. I can't find her anywhere, and the clothes in her closet are on the floor. She pulled everything in her drawers out. She pulled everything in your drawers out. She tore up the beds I had made in the morning. Everything is on the floor, all the comforters, your mother's stuff that was still in the drawers, the sheets on your parents' bed, I haven't gone in that room in years, everything torn up. She used the two toilets and didn't flush them. She was upset about her hair. I told her I was sorry she cut her braids. She didn't seem sorry. I don't understand how she could cut it, after all these years. Now you can see how crooked her eyes go, more than when she had the braids, and she looks older, you can see it now."

Ollie put a hand up to stop her stream of words. He raced up the stairs. It was true. His parents' room was pulled apart as if a professional burglar had been looking for jewels. There was a terrible mess in his room. In Sally's room it was worse. The chair was turned over. The curtains had been pulled down. In the bathroom he found his shaving cream in the tub and the mirror was smeared, a brown smear of familiar origins. In the sink leftover antibiotics from his last gum infection had mingled with spilled green mouthwash: the medicine pellets had melted into dark bleeding spots of orange.

"She must be around," said Ollie as he passed Mrs. Roomey in the front hall. "Did you tell her that her hair would grow back?" he asked.

"She didn't ask me," said Mrs. Roomey.

"I'm going to look for her. You stay here, in case she comes home."

"She didn't run away because of her hair, I know her. She wouldn't just because she had cut her hair," said Mrs. Roomey.

Rushing now, energy returned, adrenaline running, he hurried to his truck. He would find her. She couldn't have gone far: a temper tantrum, nothing more. He understood. It was Leah. It was Leah in his bed. His gratitude to a fate that had brought Leah to West Pine and finally to his bed, so that he didn't have to sleep alone, had driven Sally away. Of course she wouldn't see Leah as he did. He was right not to have Leah move in too quickly. He would have to make it up to both of them. He took the pickup down the street and around the corner. He rode back and forth on the nearby roads. He went to the playground behind the elementary school where sometimes he went with Sally at the end of the day and she pushed the swings. She was too big to sit on them but she liked to push them, back and forth. There was a large pine at the edge of the playground. Sally liked to sit under it and look up at the sky.

Ollie parked his truck and ran. "Sally," he called. It was getting dark. He felt a tension in his chest, in his shoulders. "Sally," he called, forcing his voice into a calm reassuring sound. He didn't find her. He drove along the main road. He blew his horn furiously at the car in front of him. He put

his head out the window and shouted, "You bastard,
where'd you learn to drive, Istanbul?" Sally knew she was
not supposed to go beyond the corner alone. She didn't
clearly understand about the lights, red and green, and
there was one light on the street there. In the summer the
cars waited at that corner to turn on the road that led to the
ocean. Sometimes she was patient when crossing the street
and sometimes she wasn't. Sometimes she rushed ahead
and other times she was so frightened of the cars that he
had to pull her across when the light was in their favor.

Darkness was coming. He pulled the pickup back into
his own driveway. Mrs. Roomey was in the house. She had
turned on the lights even though it was early still. She
shook her head as he approached. "Look in the cellar?" he
asked her. She nodded. Then he thought he knew. He went
into the pantry and took out an old key on a huge metal
loop. It was for the abandoned store. He walked to the front
of the property. There were no sounds in the store. The window was boarded up. Sally had cried the day he had the
board put up, but the glass had cracked and he didn't want
to replace it. He didn't want the store to look as if it might
open again. The door seemed not to have been touched but
maybe Sally had opened it, maybe she had a way of getting
in, maybe she had pushed in through the rotten boards at
the back, at the extension where his father had stored old
catalogues.

He turned the key and pushed open the door. It was dark
and musty and there was a stale smell of animal and mold.
He left the door open behind him. "Sally," he called. Holding his flashlight ahead of him the way a blind man moves
his cane, he looked behind the old counter. He let the light
slide over the long-ago-emptied shelves. He hurried as fast
as he could, avoiding the countertop, a torn-out pipe, and a

cane chair that had long ago lost its seat, into the storage area where his father had kept the boxes of nails and the cartons of wires and tubing and plumbing parts. He thought he heard the sound of wings, the flight of bats. His hands began to shake. "Sally," he called again. His voice still calm. His heart racing. She wasn't there either. He should not have been in bed with Leah. His incompetence swept over him, drying his tongue, sagging his muscles. He had not done well.

He went back to the house and called the town police. Soon after a patrol car arrived, its red light swirling about. The neighbors came. No, they hadn't seen her all day. Yesterday she had been sitting on the front porch, just sitting in her winter coat with her hands jammed in her pockets. Today they hadn't seen her at all.

The chief of police, who had been a year ahead of Ollie in school, arrived. His kid had been in Ollie's honors class. "Don't worry," said Captain Michael. "We'll find her." Ollie was pacing up and down, standing up, sitting down, shoving his hands in his pockets, pressing them together, tugging at his nose, buttoning and unbuttoning his jacket. "She doesn't understand about the cars, how fast they come," he said. "She's afraid of the dark. She likes to eat every few hours," he repeated again and again.

He called Leah.

Ollie said, "Sally's run away." There was a pause, a long pause.

Leah said, "Where would she go?"

Ollie said, "Not far. The police are looking for her."

Leah said, "I'm sorry."

Ollie said, "It's not your fault."

Leah said, "I know."

Ollie said, "I wish you were here."

Leah said, "I could come over."

Ollie said, "I'm going to go out and look again."

Leah said, "Do you want me to come?" There was a long silence. Leah almost put the phone down. She could hear her heart beat, there was a tightness in her chest.

Ollie said, "Come." Then he added, "Please come."

"Was it about her hair?" Leah asked.

Ollie wanted to say, I don't know, maybe, leave me alone, what does it matter why, I don't want to talk to you. But he just shrugged.

Leah considered. There were two policemen in the kitchen. They had found a package of brownie mix and were making brownies. She had to explain to the sergeant why she was there. "I'm his friend," she had said. "A friend of the family," she had added. But what was she, really? She thought of saying to Ollie, I'm going back to the city soon. I want to go back to work. She rehearsed it once or twice in her head. Then she didn't want to say it, not aloud, not now. This wasn't the time. She thought of saying, I'm not moving in with you ever. I don't need you. I enjoyed our friendship very much, but it was always a passing adventure. She imagined leaning over to peck him on the cheek, the way a favorite aunt might say good-bye to a visiting nephew. So glad you could come, another time, I hope. She sat down and curled her legs under her. They seemed too long. She had to get back to her lab. Tomorrow she would go. She didn't belong here, in this house.

"Has she done this before?" she asked.

"No," he said. "Never."

"She'll probably come back by herself," said Captain Michael, "most runaways do." Mrs. Roomey went home. The police cars came and went. Captain Michael spoke on his radio unit, all-points bulletin, check the beach, check the lake. The night was filled with stars. The Milky Way rolled down over the sky, glittering and sparkling. An airplane crossed to the left of the Big Dipper, its red beacon light flickering. The coast guard plane was called in from the airport. Its small motor made a roaring noise overhead. It was used in the summertime to look for sharks in the water so that the bathers could be warned in time. Now it was using a large searchlight to look for Sally along the beach.

She can't have gone far. She has a limp. She must have stopped to rest somewhere. She didn't take money. She probably got lost and can't find her way back. The men in the house talked soothingly to Ollie. They shouted a bit as if he might be deaf or as if it were he whose mind was not altogether as sharp as it might be. His face was drawn and tight. He had nothing to say to Leah. He tried to sit near her but then he would jump up and move to the other side of the room. Leah brought him a piece of cold chicken that Mrs. Roomey had left behind. He didn't touch it.

He looked at Leah sitting on the couch, her long hair not quite brushed, her dark eyes staring at him in alarm, alarm for Sally, alarm for him, alarm for herself. Leah's legs were tucked under her. Her head was back, he could see the slope of her throat. He felt no desire. She stood up, stretched her arms up over her head. She was too tall, he decided. Women shouldn't be so tall. As she turned toward the window he saw the underside of her chin, the flesh was not tight, she was getting old. He turned his head away.

"It's not your fault," said Leah.

"No," said Ollie.

"No," said Leah. "Do you want me to stay?" she said. Ollie was silent.

"Is there something I can do?" said Leah.

He didn't answer her.

"Ollie," said Leah, "talk to me."

"I feel like the goddamned fish," he said. His voice was flat, echoed oddly down his throat.

"What fish?" said Leah.

"Hemingway's fish, the one that was tied to the boat, hooked, speared, eaten by sharks, no good to anyone."

"I don't think you're supposed to identify with the fish," said Leah.

"You're a Hemingway expert?" said Ollie.

"The way you pity yourself, you're pitiful," said Leah.

"I've never pitied myself," Ollie yelled.

"Good," Leah yelled back.

"I've taken everything. Given up everything, I've done what I should." He was yelling.

Leah said without kindness, "You did."

Ollie let out a sound, a wail that came from deep in the center of his diaphragm, a sound that was rumbling, weeping, blasting, howling, baying, primal, terrible, frightened and frightening, man before he learned to garden or play chess, when he was half an ape, a hairy beast who could imagine his own death, but neither made nor extinguished fires. It brought tears to Ollie's eyes, that he could make a sound like that. Leah was still. She recognized the sound. Maybe the fish, tied to the boat, made a sound like that, underwater where nobody could hear.

He thought of Sally out alone in the dark.

"She needs me," he said.

"I know," said Leah.

I have to do something, he thought to himself. "I'm a mess," he said to Leah.

"You are," said Leah.

He wanted to touch Leah's face with his hand but he didn't.

"Fool, stupid fool," he said.

"Who?" said Leah. If he meant her she was going to leave, leave permanently.

"Me," said Ollie. "Me."

Leah said, "We'll go look. I'll drive, you direct me."

He looked for the car keys he had thrown on the kitchen counter behind the milk bottle and forgotten. He found them. He moved like a man half-asleep into the truck. "God," he said. "She must be afraid. She's waiting for me somewhere." His voice was a dead weight. It sank into the night. "Thank you for coming with me," said Ollie very formally, very slowly, as if he were an earthquake victim talking to a Red Cross representative who didn't understand the local dialect.

Leah and Ollie went to the beach. Ollie went to the left. Leah went to the right. They each had a flashlight. In the dark, with the clouds covering most of the stars, their two lights made an arc, moving away from each other, like airplanes moving in opposite directions across the sky.

Leah walked along the dunes, shining her flashlight up into the grasses, over the sign that said Danger: Disease-Carrying Ticks. She looked ahead of her where the driftwood logs had formed a kind of seat, a bench on which to view the comings and the goings of the tide. It was bitter cold. She zipped her parka up over her neck and pulled her hat down over her ears. The coast guard plane flew over the beach, low down, its lights on the water, expecting what? Leah saw a dark object ahead. She hurried toward it. A cap, someone's cap. It was caked with sand and a ball of seaweed had caught in the wet wool. It was not Sally's cap. Sally had a red and white cap with reindeer on the side.

The police four-wheel-drive jeeps left the parking lot and roared onto the beach, their lights reflected up onto the horizon's edge, diffused into the dark somewhere beyond the slope of the earth, light filtered through the sky as if headed for Spain. The wide ocean lurched back and forth. The sky reached out over them all. The lights of the jeeps swept everything clean in front of the vehicles. Nothing was in their way, no human form showed up, logs, flat sand, dunes, the beach houses up a few miles, now hulking shapes, silhouettes in the moonlight, patient as their owners slept elsewhere. An abandoned umbrella, rusted and torn, was caught in the chicken wire that protected the dunes.

The spray from the sea whipped in Leah's face. "Sally," she called every few steps as she swept her flashlight in an arc that included all of the beach, dune to wave, in a slow-motion swing. Her fingers felt numb. She felt a dread that was Ollie's dread. Sally's disappearance had consequences, an alteration of the design that would change everything after. What was Ollie without Sally? For a moment hope ran like an electric shock through every bone in her body. Ollie will be free. But he wouldn't be free. Hope subsided, leaving behind traces of shame. He would be even more bound. I'm free, she thought. I'm free to leave. This did not make her happy. Leah considered the cord that bound her to Ollie and the cord that bound Ollie to Sally and the cords that bound the three of them together. In the range of the entire galaxy, the enormity of the ocean, the distance of the horizon, what did it matter whom she loved or who loved her, or what happened to her or what happened to him or what happened to his sister? Who cared? She had tears in her eyes: maybe they came from the wind blowing right in her face. "Sally," she called out, raising her flashlight over her head and losing its light in the Milky Way. Damn, where are you? Then a mile and a half down the beach she turned back. It was enough. She had tried hard enough.

Ollie walked swiftly, taking ten steps toward the dunes and then ten steps down to the water. He swung his flashlight up and down. He saw the dark ocean banging against the shore. He thought of bats. There were no bats by the ocean. His hands were cold. The just-healed blister on his palm ached. He thought of Leah. He headed back to the parking lot. He found her waiting for him by the pickup. She shook her head. He shook his. They got in the truck. They drove to the Senior Citizens' Center. It was dark, locked, closed. They walked around it, shining their lights behind the evergreen hedges. It would have been far for her to walk. "Sally," they called. She wasn't there.

She drove past the Sonnabend house. The light was on in the kitchen. Leah pulled the truck into the driveway. Litzie came to the door. André in his bathrobe stood behind her. Had they seen her? Ollie asked. They hadn't.

"My sister is capable of anything," he said.

"They'll find her," said Litzie.

"It's my fault," said Ollie.

"I doubt it," said Litzie.

They made noises of comfort, snorts of concern, they were friends. The ice of Leah's fright began to thaw, exposing a rawness she hadn't herself seen. "Ollie," she said and couldn't continue because the words weren't there. She had a complaint, a roaring complaint, but she couldn't find the way to say it. "Ollie," she said, "we have to keep looking."

André was tired. The circles under his eyes were deep. He had just settled in bed with a copy of the *Psychoanalytic*

Quarterly on his lap. It would have put him to sleep within minutes. André put on his coat. He put on his hat with the earflaps and his scarf and his leather gloves and he took his flashlight and went out in the night, down to the beach to join the police in their search.

The police pulled their jeep up to the abandoned coast guard station. During the Second World War it had been used as the center of operations for the eastern end of the shore. Then boats had patrolled the waters twenty-four hours a day, binoculars scanned the monotonous waves as young men drained their eyesight looking for enemy periscopes, landing craft, that would come up from the ocean floor with the weeds and the mussel shells and the tiny half-formed scallops. Now a relic of the last good war, the building was plastered with signs, Keep Out, Danger, Faulty Boards, The Town of West Pine Not Responsible for Personal Safety, but the teenagers, decade after decade, had broken in, found ways to unpadlock the rusty, algae-encrusted padlock, and commit those sins that mark the edges of adulthood. A few babies were conceived in the dank bunk beds with their bug-infested mattresses, now flattened and moist. Those babies themselves had grown up and left Twinkie wrappers, Camel cigarettes, condoms used and unused, on the old coast guard station's now buckling floor.

The police headlights shone on the locked door. There were four of them. The men had trouble with the lock. They had a key but everything was rusted, and brine and darkness made it difficult. Finally they swung their bodies against the door and it gave way. They walked through the building. "Nobody yet," said the sergeant into his walkie-talkie. With their feet they pushed aside piles of old newspaper. They walked through the large room that once held the ship-to-shore radio receiver, the desk with the logbook. There was a scurrying along the floor as a family of voles rushed for the darker area in the room behind.

A terrible smell of something dead came from behind the metal staircase that led to the second floor. A policeman, so young that he still shaved every other day, so earnest that his shoulders never settled down into their sockets while he was on duty, his neck muscles taut with eagerness, shone his flashlight there on a cat, flattened fur, eyes without shape, decay in the paws and the twisted haunches. The young policeman felt nausea rise in his belly. He fought it back. He felt light-headed. "Fucking dead cat back here," he called out. "No sign of the woman," he said. He hurried upstairs, flashed his light around the floor. The shuttered windows made the area darker and more alien. "Christ," he said, "it's cold." The wind blew against the side of the building and the window frames rattled, their broken shards had long ago fallen across the floor. The young policeman crunched something hard beneath his boot. He shone his flashlight down and the light reflected off a puddle of freshly broken glass. "Christ," he repeated. He went back down the stairs and out the back.

Down the beach the men approached the shack that housed the lifeguard equipment for the Silver Head and Indian Pebble beaches. There the shack door was swinging open. Inside were the three high lifeguard chairs pressed next to each other, the ropes and the life preservers and the Styrofoam rocket-shaped buoys that were used to mark off the protected area during the season. The woman was not hiding in the shack. But as the young policeman shone his light into the small structure he saw the way the sand had been smoothed by something oval sliding down toward the

black expanse of open sea. "Here," he called, forcing the
excitement out of his voice, "I found something." There on
the floor in the dust was a red wool glove, clean and dry.

The sergeant came over. He looked at the smooth track of
the object that they followed down to the water. There were
prints, had to be recent boots. "The raft, the plastic raft that
we keep here, after the summer, she must have taken it."
The young policeman tried to hold his voice steady, professional, as if every day he had a part in a life-and-death
drama. The men went back into the shack. There on the far
wall where the raft intended to aid the lifeguards in the
summer, intended for approach to boats anchored offshore,
not intended to beard the sea, not a boat at all but a play-
thing, a toy for exercising upper-arm muscles, for storing on
the foredeck of boats that you didn't really expect to run
into trouble, a boat that was used by the lifeguards to practice rescuing swimmers, were only a pair of black plastic
oars. In the shadow cast by the flashlights they could see a
green spongy fungus growing on the life preservers. There
where the raft should have been they found a mark on the
wall surrounded by old dust: a huge broken cobweb dangled from the top of an oar. The light made the clear area
shine as if it were wet. The raft was not there. The woman
must have stolen it.

The men looked at each other, a retarded woman in an
orange plastic boat with no oars, at sea, at night. The sergeant used his radio. The young policeman sighed. He
wanted to be the one to find the woman. Nothing ever
happened to him. The last DWI arrest was made by the other
rookie. There had been a burglary and vandalism arrest just
two weeks before but he had been home nursing an ankle he
had sprained while playing Frisbee with his older brother in
the backyard. There had been a fight in front of the movie

theater, two high school girls pulling each other's hair, the previous Saturday night, but he had just felt awkward standing between them. On the beach their jeep waited, its tires set to drive along the sand, its headlights on, and the light shone down the beach showing darkness and flatness, sand and log, ridges in which seaweed and shells sank, dune grass bending. The moon halfway over the sky was irregular-shaped, a face after dental surgery, the stars were hidden. The wind blew harder, making it difficult to move forward, the men hunched down, pushed against the sheet of wind. "What made her run?" asked the sergeant as they moved, swinging their flashlights in wide arcs slowly along the edge of the shore. "Her brother's got a girlfriend," said the young policeman.

Sally had pushed the orange raft off the shore. She had climbed in, getting her boots full of sand, getting her overalls wet up to her calves. The cold stung. She had lain down on her stomach and pushed at the bottom with her arms, getting her sleeves wet. She licked the salt off her lips and wiped her face with her arm. The orange boat, a bathtub of plastic, was caught on a rising wave and pulled with the tidal surge out a few yards, and then a few more. Once it was afloat, moving out into the darkness on the swells of the waves, which were not so heavy as they might have been, not so gentle either, she leaned back in the boat and stretched out her legs and looked at the sky. She only had one glove. Ollie would be mad she lost a glove. Who cares. Ollie would come and find her. Or he wouldn't. She was not afraid, or angry anymore. She felt tired and peaceful. The way she did after a long night of watching TV. She could see the moon. The cold hurt her hand without the glove. Her wool hat slipped to one side. She straightened it. Maybe she would sail to her mother, her mother was somewhere up in the sky, Mrs. Roomey had said so, Ollie said no, but somewhere she must be, her father too. My Olive Oyl, he would say, my Minnie Mouse, he would whisper in her ear, his breath hot on her neck and his unshaved chin prickling against her face. Her mother was out there. Sally was not afraid, she was beyond the crashing of waves and out in the lilting rising sea, darkness all around. It was all right. She was not afraid. Ollie would be afraid. Where was she? He would be afraid. She almost felt sad for him. The dish ran away with the spoon, the cow jumped over the moon, the owl and the pussycat went to sea in a pea green boat, she remembered something, something like that.

There she was, a heavy woman with a square jaw, with eyes that didn't move in tandem, with a tongue that made odd forward thrusts that sometimes interfered with her speech, a woman with folds of flesh around her hips, and her body hidden behind her overalls seemed a burden that she lifted, up and down, with the motion of the waves. There she was with the whole sky above her, and beneath her the night sea, with its feeding and drifting, its dividing and dying, in the whole of the universe no eye was upon her. She drifted on, a pinpoint of self, subject to gravity, to time, to accident, to the actions of others, to the voice within, the voice that repeated over and over, The owl and the pussycat went to sea, in a pea green boat. Now she had a man's haircut, like her father, now she had no braids, now she was a man. She drifted outward, toward day, toward the horizon, where the sea stopped and the sky began.

The coast guard had two boats patrolling the water off the beach. They knew she couldn't be far. Their lights swept the water in arcs forward and back. If the boat didn't turn over, if the ocean didn't suddenly turn fierce, they would find her soon. She had to be there. They figured the currents, they knew the depths and the drift, they took a while coming out of the bay, but now they were in the area, close to shore, off the West Pine beaches, Silver Head and Indian Pebble, quietly looking: young men, woken from sleep.

Ollie and Leah went to the small pond just behind St. Peter's Church at the corner. It was a deep pond made by the discarded piece of a passing glacier some billion years before. In the summer children splashed in the water and frogs sang by the edge and the mud was black as tar. Ollie and Leah pushed their way through the brush. They held their flashlights high. "Sally," they called till they came to the edge where a red plastic shovel testified to the activities of the warmer seasons. The pond was dark and the water was still. March winds blew. The dirt was hard and the branches that stretched across the ground were dry and stiff. Leah wanted to reach for Ollie's hand but he seemed to be behind a wall, a place she could not go. He was imagining Sally's body floating at the bottom, tangled in the stems of the water lilies that bloomed each August, stones and wood drifting over it. "She's not here," he said. "Leah," he said, "there is something you don't know."

"There are a lot of things I don't know," said Leah.

"God," said Ollie. "You don't have to smart mouth me."

"You're not gay. I know you're not gay," said Leah.

"It's not that," said Ollie.

"What is it, then?" said Leah.

"I've never told anyone," said Ollie.

"You don't have to tell me," said Leah.

"Yes, I do," said Ollie.

"Now?" said Leah.

"Later," said Ollie. He looked pale. He looked ill. He put

his hand on her shoulder. He pulled her close. He wrapped his arms around her. He wanted to keep the wind off her back. She could hear his heart beating. Leah wanted to wrap him up, carry him away, protect him, find his sister for him.

She said, "We'll talk about it later." They went back to the road. A cruising police car stopped. Word had just come over the police radio. A red glove was found. A raft was missing. It looked like the woman had dragged it down to the water.

It was after midnight. There had been no new information for hours. The captain had reassured him, the coast guard had the right equipment on board. Mrs. Roomey had said that Sally was wearing her parka, her heavy overalls. It would be all right, they would have her returned within hours.

Ollie had gone silent. He had said nothing for a long time. They had gone to the beach to wait. They were in the parking lot in the pickup truck. Ollie listed to one side, leaned his head against the window. He seemed to sleep. He wasn't asleep. Leah listened to the radio, the weather, the news, the local deejay, who was pushing a band that was playing next Friday in East Pine. She didn't want to move in with Ollie. She wasn't sure she even liked Ollie. She didn't care if he cared about her. She knew what mattered to her. Work, and more work. Love, as she had always suspected, was a leash, a burden, a fraud, a crime committed by the soul against itself. She would tell him as soon as Sally was found, she would explain that it was over. So he had a secret, and she was expected to mind, a wife, a mistress, a child or two, a disease, a bank account in Switzerland, a love affair with a married woman.

A soreness overcame her, an ache hit her. She was a person who would never, this was the last chance, who would never be part of a twosome. She would be her own seesaw partner, rising and sinking, up and down, on the board alone. She should have known better than to believe in miracles. She who was born understanding how little there was to get, how little safety there was, how wary one had to be, glancing over the shoulder, checking everything out, giving your hand to someone only if necessary, how easy it was for the rug to be pulled out, how could she be surprised when she found herself midair, falling?

The orange boat had a rope hanging off its rounded front. The rope floated through the water with the boat. The rope caught a log, the log was pushed down under the next wave, the boat dipped down too. Sally felt the water up over her hips. She decided to close her eyes. She had stared at the moon long enough. The current carried her onward along the slope of the coast, the winds blew northeast, the tide was coming in, the curve of the land bulged and contracted. The fish of the deep drifted forward and backward in the streams of the foam and churned-up sand.

Ollie looked at Leah without a change in expression. He seemed far away and his skin was gray. His eyes were empty. He seemed to be sitting there simply breathing, in and out, in and out. Leah watched the headlights of the cars shine on the waves, as if they were on a movie set. The tide was coming in. Sally might be pushed ashore, but where on the long beach? There were two coast guard boats out looking, jeeps riding along the strip of sand, the search plane was flying low above the beaches.

Leah said, "It's not your fault."

Ollie said, "Funny you should say that."

"What do you mean?" Leah said.

Ollie said, "It's just a thing people say, right, it's not your fault, as if they knew, as if they were sure, as if none of us had any responsibility for what happened, as if the gods or God were pulling all the strings."

Leah was surprised. She was quiet. She looked at him. She considered telling him she was going back to the city. She waited.

"It's like a mantra," he went on. "It's not your fault, it's not my fault, I didn't do it, I'm not to blame. It's what Cain said to God when he found him standing over the body of Abel. 'Who, me? Not me.' "

"I only meant," said Leah, "that Sally was upset. That she doesn't understand is not your fault. You've been such a good brother, so many years."

"Have I?" said Ollie. His voice was flat, hard, wooden.

"I think I'm going back to the city," said Leah.

"What do you know about fault?" said Ollie.

"You've taken care of her, like she was your child," said Leah. "That's good of you. I think you're a good man."

"You do?" said Ollie. "I tell my kids when we read *The Scarlet Letter*, I tell them to be suspicious of respectable types. The better people act, the worse they are. The goody-goody ones, charitable, modest, pure, that's where the blood is . . ."

Leah had to lean forward to hear him. His voice seemed to come out of a deep spot in the center of his chest; a rumble, a wind rattling through a distant mountain pass. Leah thought about the weather. The temperature was sure to drop further in the coming hours as the next front moved in. She hadn't heard the news but she expected that the freezing point would be reached before dawn. There were probably snow clouds in Wisconsin and maybe rain in Florida. She considered the globe with the flow of wind and air, rising and falling pressures, clouds sinking and disappearing, it gave her comfort. Her bones were heavy.

"I don't want to hear your secret," said Leah.

"All right," said Ollie.

"Maybe you should tell me," said Leah. There was silence in the truck. The engine hummed. It was the kind of silence in which you could hear the dune grass bending. The ocean continued to rock in its huge basin.

"Do you know," said Leah, "that the ocean was formed by the motion of the earth's tectonic plates?"

Ollie said, "I'm tired, tired of everything. I'm too tired to talk."

Leah said, "I'm going soon, I'm going back to the city."

Ollie heard her. He could feel his pulse throb in a vein in his forehead, a stroke, a heart attack, the approach of pain. He didn't care. He did not want to be alone. He wanted her to stay. He closed his eyes and turned his head away from her. She put her hand on the door. She might not have been planning to open it. She might have. He opened his eyes. His neck tensed. Ollie said, "It is my fault."

Leah wasn't sure whether he meant Sally's disappearance, her going back to the city, something else. "What do you mean?" she said. He gasped like a fish landed on the deck. He took the chance.

He told her.

Solomon Marcus, Sol to his friends, had always been able to do things with his hands. Jews weren't supposed to be fixers and menders, but he was. Even as a boy in Flatbush he had made shelves for his mother out of milk cartons. He had made a table for his cousin for her wedding. He knew about saws and nails and carpenter's levels that kept lines straight even though the earth was curved. He was patient. You needed to be patient and steady to plane and nail, to sandpaper rough edges, to paint and screw. He could fix wires and sockets, radios and watches. He was that kind of man. So when he was ready to throw out the baby carriage that had once held Ollie and then Sally, because the springs had rusted, because the mattress had green mold in the corners, because he wasn't going to need it anymore, it was natural that he would remove the wheels and make his daughter a wagon, a red wagon to pull her dolls in. He made it in the basement, where he kept his tools. Ollie would sit on the cellar steps and watch his father carefully measure and cut, nail and hammer. His father went down into the cellar early in the morning before the first customer. While his wife was fixing up the display pot holders that hung on a string, while she was arranging the light bulbs, 40, 60, 100 watts, in separate piles that were stacked on the back shelves, he would go downstairs and work on the wagon for his daughter. He worked under a single bare light that dangled from a chain attached to a pipe on the ceiling. He had a radio down in the cellar. It would play music, dance music, and often Sol Marcus would sing along, or hum, and occasionally he would bang on the table, following the rhythms of the band. Ollie listened to the announcer who would interrupt every fifteen minutes and in a deep smooth voice offer advice about razors and shaving cream, soap and laxatives, toothpaste and hair creams.

Ollie watched. The wagon began as bare planks. Slowly it took shape. "Can I help?" he asked. "Not yet," said his father. Sally was going to have her fifth birthday in a few weeks. The relatives were coming from Brooklyn. Sally had long hair that her mother plaited in braids each morning.

Her eyes were clear, like the noon sky over the ocean on a cloudless day. She had a Raggedy Ann doll with a candy heart that she carried with her wherever she went. She had sturdy legs that were sometimes scratched because she liked to climb the apple tree in their backyard. "I'm up here," she would call out, "no one can reach me, I'm so big, bigger than anyone." She slept under a quilt her mother had made for her that had an elephant at the center and tigers walking around the edges. Every week Miriam Marcus would walk her two children to the library on Main Street and they would take out new books. Sally could read some words. She could count to one hundred. She added with her fingers. She had a collection of acorns that she kept on her window ledge. Each acorn had a name and they were a family, an ever-growing family. She had a friend named Emily who lived three houses down. Emily and Sally would go out in the yard and catch caterpillars and put them in jars, waiting for them to turn into butterflies.

Ollie's seventh birthday had passed and his mother had made him a cake. He had wanted a train. He had wanted an electric train that ran around tracks with signal lights, a station house, fences that went down with little bells. He had seen such a train in the store at Christmastime. It was sold. Ollie had said to his father, "I want a train like that." His father had said, "You think you're a rich kid, a kid with two houses." "No," said Ollie. "I don't." He was ashamed. He had been too big for his britches, too eager by half. "I don't want a train," he said to his mother sometime later. "Good," she said.

She was tired after working all day in the store. She went into the house and picked up her daughter and, holding her on her lap, rocked back and forth and closed her eyes. Ollie sat by her side and leaned against her leg. Once he had

touched her stocking. She had slapped his hand away. He
was a child who watched. He considered before he jumped.
He liked to draw airplanes and trains and cars on the corners of old newspaper his father let him have. He woke up
at night and went into his parents' bedroom and found
them wrapped in their quilt, arms around each other. He
watched them sleep. He went into his sister's room. She held
her doll in her arms. She slept on her stomach. If he tried to
get into bed with her she would wake and complain to his
mother. Her room smelled of sleep and warm breath, and
washed clothes. Ollie's eyes would shut during the day, at
school at his desk. Sometimes he slept on the ground under
the large maple in the schoolyard where he was sitting
watching the other children chase each other. He fell asleep
during the day and was awake at night. He was that kind of
child.

His father painted the wood planks red. He waited till
they dried. He came back down into the cellar in the evening after dinner and, with a thin white brush running over
a stencil he had made from cardboard, he wrote the word
Sally on the side of the wagon.

"So," he said to his son. "She'll like it?"

"Yes," said Ollie, "she will."

"It needs a handle," said his father, "a long handle so she
can pull it."

"I'll make the handle," said Ollie.

"No," said his father. "You can't." Too big for his britches,
he was ashamed.

In the cellar under the single bulb the wagon waited for
its handle, it waited for Solomon Marcus to finish his
daughter's birthday present. Ollie sat on the cool steps. He
heard his father above in the store and a customer walking
heavy on the floor. He heard his father drop a carton, a large

carton. He stared at the wagon with the word Sally written on its side. There was a large cobweb in the corner. The spider had wrapped up several flies for later consumption. Ollie took a stick from a pile of wood scraps and carefully walked over to the web and poked in the middle, then flung his arms upward and around till the threads of the web went spinning. The ends attached to his stick. The corpses of flies fell to the floor and the spider rose high out of reach. Upstairs they called him for dinner. He waited for them to call again. They were talking. They didn't call him. He was hungry. He went upstairs. They had started without him. "We thought you had fallen asleep," said his father. "You should come when we call," said his mother.

Then one Saturday morning just before Sally's birthday he went with his father to the town dump. There were the ditches filled with bags, orange peels, paper containers, soiled newspapers, vegetables, raw and cooked, rotting in old cans. On the far side of the ditch, rows and rows of sea gulls sat, large fat sea gulls with eyes blinking in the sun. They would move in a sudden burst of wing and breast toward the garbage, cawing to one another, pecking at each other, they would swoop and charge and retreat to the far side. Tractors that plowed the garbage into the ground moved back and forth, their plows rusty and their cabins dark, their wheel tracks stained with smears of juice and crushed chicken bones. On a small hill to one side sat the items for reuse, the old toys, the broken chairs, the soggy cushions, the games with pieces missing, the lamps with cracked bases that had been thrown out by West Pine citizens. It was in this pile that Sol Marcus and his son went looking for something that would make a good handle for a red wagon, a gift for a little girl who was about to have her fifth birthday.

Here Sol Marcus found it. It was an old croquet mallet with red and white stripes and a wooden handle.

"This will do," he said.

"How will you attach it?" asked Ollie.

"I'll figure it out," said his father. They brought the mallet home and took it down to the cellar. Then Sol Marcus had to relieve his wife at the store. His wife went into the house to vacuum with the loud heavy Hoover that a customer had returned the year before, to do the laundry, which she still did by hand in the bathtub on the ground floor.

Sally said to Ollie, "I want to go down to the cellar and see what Daddy is making for me."

"No," said Ollie, "it's a surprise."

"I don't want it to be a surprise," said Sally. "I want to see it now. I'm going." She opened the cellar door. She went down the stairs. Ollie followed her. He could have called his mother then. He could have gone into the store and called his father then. He didn't. He followed her down the stairs. He pulled the chain to turn on the light.

Here Ollie paused in his story. His breathing was shallow. Leah was listening quietly. She could tell from the urgency in his voice, the flatness of tone, the way his muscles bulged in his neck, that the story had meaning, it had plot, though so far she didn't see it, at all. He seemed to have a lump in his throat. He coughed. He steadied himself.

Sally saw the wagon. "My wagon," she said. "My name," she crowed when she saw the white writing on the side. "My beautiful wagon," she said and Ollie was sad. How is a child sad? Ollie did not feel like the cellar was his cellar anymore. Not the place where his father worked and listened to the radio, it was something else, a place in a dream, a place with dark creatures in corners, with poison seeping from cracks in the wall, a place like the bottom of a well from which you might not emerge, you might drift downward forever. "My wagon," she cried. "You may never, never use it, you may never, never touch it. It's mine." She clasped her hands together and on her tiptoes began a kind of dance, a sort of happy skip. She curled her lips at him. "He never made you a wagon, did he?" she said. Then she turned her back on him. It was in that second that he picked up the mallet and swung it twice over his head and as he was swinging it he wanted to stop, to direct his hands somewhere else, but the motion had started and he couldn't stop it, and he let his arms follow down smoothly. He hadn't thought about hitting her. He hadn't intended to make her fall down, but she did. There was blood coming from the back of her head. There was blood on the mallet.

Ollie was white as a sheet as he told Leah this last part. His words had come slowly. How does a child feel when he has done something he knows is wrong, very wrong, will change everything ever after? His stomach hurts, his eyes ache. He feels like he needs to be held. He runs up the stairs to his mother and forces her to stop what she's doing, to take her arms covered with soap and embrace him, to get up from her knees and follow him down to the cellar where his sister is lying, like a doll abandoned at the dump, with matted hair and something wrong, something wrong with her.

Ollie was quiet. Leah could hear her own heart beat. "You made this up," she said. "You felt guilty and you made this up."

"No," said Ollie, "I have never told anyone, but I've never lied to myself either. I have never pretended to myself that it was something else, the way my mother wanted me to do. I have never pretended. This is a secret, a thirty-six-year-old secret.

"They told the doctors at the hospital that she fell down the cellar steps and, slipping, hit her head on the back edge of the stair. They told the neighbors she had fallen. They told the school that I was so upset about my sister's fall that I had to be excused for the rest of the year. They told me not to tell, not anyone, ever. They would say I was lying and I would be put away, taken away to a place like jail or worse, a hospital for the criminally insane. Was I insane? Can a seven-year-old-boy who loses his temper for a moment be criminally insane? I don't know. They didn't punish me. My mother said it was an accident. My father said it was his fault for leaving the mallet there, not attaching it imme- diately to the wagon.

"For a long time my sister was in the hospital. At first the doctors thought maybe it would be all right, that slowly she would recover completely. Each day after work, after the store closed, they would drive to the hospital and I would wait at home. I wanted to go with them but they didn't want me. They let me wait at the window watching for their re- turn. I was told not to put on the lights because they didn't want to spend the extra money, so I waited in the dark. I was afraid of robbers and kidnappers, of aliens and snakes, and of course bats. I was a child, after all."

"Of course you were a child," said Leah.

"They brought her home," said Ollie, "with her eyes changed, a little out of focus like now, with her tongue dart- ing out of her mouth and her words not clear. She had a limp. Some kind of damage somewhere in the skull. She carried her Raggedy Ann doll around. She followed my mother in and out of the store. She grew in her body but not in her mind. My mother said I was to take care of her. My father said it was my responsibility, for the rest of my life, and I have — I have taken care of her." Ollie's eyes stared at Leah, not quite seeing her, like a boy in the midst of a dream. There were tears. They slipped down his cheeks, and fogged his glasses. "So you know what I am," he said. His voice was weak, flat, drained. It scraped across his vocal cords like the voice of a very old man.

His muscles quivered. His head was tucked down. He was resigned. He had told. It was strange to have said it aloud, the weight was still there, doubled perhaps by the knowledge that his secret was now shared, his revulsion echoed, its truth mirrored in the mind of this woman who was after all a stranger.

He had pushed her away. Now she would go. He had wanted and not wanted to be free of her. He had been trespassing, masquerading as a man who could when he couldn't, who had a right to what he didn't have a right to. He had been conned into hope. He had conned her into hope. He had lost her in that dark hole of his childhood. He had lost her in that one instant, the one that replayed in his mind over and over, always with the same completion, never with his arms stopping, never with a backward step instead of a forward one, over and over, he saw it, in slow motion, in fast forward, in rewind, it never changed.

Leah was silent. It was clear, the seven-year-old boy lifting his arms, swinging the mallet, the little girl on the cellar floor, the little girl in the hospital, the parents at risk of losing two children. Never speak of it, they said, don't tell anyone. Nothing the same ever afterward. Before the accident, after the accident, they spoke of time that way, they spoke of Sally that way, before the accident and after, they spoke of themselves that way as if they too had crossed a divide, a canyon that marked their lives, before the accident and after the accident.

Ollie's mother wanted to go to her family in Brooklyn, to leave West Pine, she needed her family. Ollie's father shouted at her. He wouldn't move. He had the store. It was doing well enough. He had made a place for himself in America. He didn't want to go back where he had come from. "We have to go on," he had said. "We can't let this stop our lives." But it had anyway. Ollie's father never made anything else in his workroom, his tools got dusty, and one year the rain came in through a leak on the side of the house, and the cellar, even after it was pumped out, remained damp and musty. One morning Ollie's father chopped up the wagon for firewood. The next winter they burned the red planks in the fireplace. Sally didn't notice. She couldn't read her name anymore.

Leah had her head in her hands. Her face burned. Ollie did not look at her. That was a good thing. Only politeness prevented her from moving away, leaving him there. She thought him ugly, sweaty. His features, the set of his nose and the curve of his lips and the shape of his cheeks, were no longer pleasing to her. She noticed that he had hairs in his nostrils, deep shadows under his eyes. He had crossed some line. He had hurt someone. A man who could do that once could do anything. She felt cold. She considered, I'm going back to the city. She waited for the right moment to speak. She tried to forgive him: it wasn't this Ollie, the one in the truck with her, it was a child who had lifted the mallet, who had swung with his small arms thirty-six years ago. A man is not responsible for the boy he was. No, she changed her mind. It was this Ollie. We are ourselves all our lives. She saw now that he was one of them. Them she used to think of, dream about sometimes, coming up behind her, riding in an elevator with her, jumping out from behind a stoop, serial killers, rapists, SS commandos, men with tattoos on their arms who laughed as they tied up women, and watched as their blood ran down.

Ollie said, "Leah, I'm going to walk around. I'll leave you alone."

He put his hands on the door handle. His face had returned to itself, its puzzled, irregular, crumpled self. He tried to smile. It wasn't a real smile. It was a sort of self-conscious uncomfortable grimace, a weary smile that was mingled with distance, and came from behind a wall. It's all right, said the smile, I know I'm beyond touch, the gates have closed behind me. You have no responsibility toward me. "You understand," he said, "why I have to take care of Sally. Why I can't — "

He let the door slam behind him, letting in a burst of cold air. The coast guard boat with its swinging lights passed offshore, the police cars gathered on the sand with their headlights on, their tires rocking in new-made ruts. Sorrow seeped into her bones. So she sat for a while, playing the story over and over in her head, that was his secret, that was his secret, she told it to herself, sparing no detail, imagining it all. It sank into her further and further, gooseflesh on her arms, a rasp in her breath. A child, she told herself, a young child, jealous child, a child, she said to herself as the repulsion surged and subsided in a rhythm of its own. The facts of the story floated in her mind, fractured her thoughts, forced their way like shards of a broken glass straight through her. That he had done it, was capable of it, seemed both impossible and possible. Could she have? If she had a brother? Could she have? No, yes, maybe. No. She was better off alone. Alone without a man she would be safe. "Safe" she considered and with the word came a hollowness, a dread, a new dread. Trust someone, she said to herself, but who? She thought of her mother, staring up at the ceiling, lying in bed, leaving the sheets wet with her sweat, more flesh than spirit, bone and vessel, forgetting about her daughter, not needing her daughter, not knowing that her daughter had called her name. Trust someone, she said to herself. Leah stood on the edge of decision, she backed up and down, she let the weight of his story and her story clash and merge and rise and sink, and she thought of herself in the days ahead, without him, with him, without him alone like a shell on the beach, picked dry, with him something else, maybe. Brave, she scaled the walls of herself and broke free.

She got out of the truck and found Ollie talking to a policeman halfway toward the shore. "Why don't you go home, Mr. Marcus," the young man was saying.

Ollie shook his head. "I'll wait." Leah came behind him and gently touched his shoulder. He turned. "Do you want me to take you home?" he asked. Behind his glasses, his eyes blinked. There were drops in his hair from the spray of the waves.

Need had driven her to the brink. Courage carried her over. A gale force pushed her, she had lost caution, good and bad, safe and unsafe, order and reason had vanished. Her careful considerations of moments before were gone, swept off in the cleansing fires of affection that now burned and roared and cast a glorious new light along the corridors of her mind. For the first time she understood Héloïse, she understood Juliet. She understood them all, Hera the scorned, Helen of Troy, women who waited, women who followed, women who wouldn't give up, women who knew what she now knew: Rosalind, Kate, even Desdemona. Despite reason, despite everything, Leah placed her arms around his body and held tight, tighter than she had ever held on to anyone before. He was stiff beneath her grasp. "Are you going away?" he asked her. The young policeman was embarrassed and hurried back to his jeep.

"I'm not going anywhere without you," she said. She put her fingers up to his mouth. "It's enough," she said. "It's been long enough." She heard herself say the words. She was surprised. A few moments ago she had wanted to leave. She was dizzy, exhausted, flooded with desire, desire for what? She paused. She put her mouth on his mouth, put her nose next to his nose. Yes, she felt a heat rising in her breasts, but it wasn't about that. She put a hand on his chest and stroked him gently. "It happened a long time ago," she said. "You were a child."

There were tears in his eyes now. "I know," he said. "Stay," he said.

"I will," she said.

"Are you going to change your mind?" he asked.

"Are you going to change yours?" she asked.

"You forgive me?" he said.

"Forgive yourself," she said.

"I've been trying," he said.

"Try harder," she said.

"Are you staying?" he said.

"I said so," she said.

"Say it again," he said. She did.

They were together back in the car, his arms and her arms, his face and her face, her legs and his legs, close but not touching, staring out the window at the black edge of the sea. The few stars pulsed in the darkness, a plane crossed over the sky on its way toward India. They said nothing. The fear of loss hung over them. Sally was out there on the sea. They waited. But time was passing and time was not on Sally's side. Ollie drove the car a few miles down the road and they walked across the park reserve to the beach, down an access road on the far side of the lighthouse to a place where the land curved outward and the tides rode high.

The current moved fast. The cold air blew on the ocean. The dark waves lifted themselves up and sank back down, one after the other. A shooting star crossed the far horizon and disappeared into the darkness. The moon turned whiter and rose higher till it crossed the center of the sky and began its downward fall toward Japan, toward the South Pole. Sally put her red leather glove, a gift from the Senior Citizens' Center on her last birthday, on the round side of her raft. The waves swelled up, her remaining glove slipped overboard. Her fingers were swollen. She put her hands in the water trying to save her glove. It sank quickly and her hands in the cold water grasped at streams of moving water. When she put her arm back in the raft it was dripping. She sucked at the drops. She was thirsty. She had had enough of the sea. The raft drifted into a shoal off the shore. It stuck on a sandbar. The water was calm before the shore. It was far down the beach, miles away from the parking lot, away from the old coast guard station, away from the lifeguard hutch. Her overalls were heavy with water. Her clothes stank of sea. Where was she? She didn't know. She wanted to go home. It was time. She put up a hand for someone to lead her home. She was alone on the water in the dark, under the moonlight. She was afraid. Of what? She was afraid of being alone. The raft rocked on the sandbar. It didn't move forward. She waited. She was good at waiting. Perhaps her mother would see that she was alone on the beach and she would come down from the sky and bring her home.

The coast guard boats swept the sea with their searchlights. They found nothing. The jeeps ran along the beach, they found nothing, not the other glove, not a footprint, nothing. The police began to knock on the doors of the occasional house that had a car in the driveway. They woke sleepy occupants — "Have you seen Sally Marcus tonight?" Most of the houses by the ocean were owned by summer people. They were locked and dark and uninhabited. Had Sally broken into one of them? Was she hiding inside? The captain, his police force, were looking in yards, on porches, inside sheds that were not securely padlocked. The young policeman was excited. His face was flushed. It was almost like television, only everything moved slower. If they were going to find a body, he hoped it would be his flashlight, his lifting of evergreen brush, his hand that uncovered the dead.

André Sonnabend had taken his car down to the point just before the lighthouse and was walking on the beach. He was swinging his flashlight in front of him. He had promised himself that he would walk about a mile in each direction, but his ears were cold, even under his wool hat, and he was thinking of returning when he caught sight of an orange form on the sandbar out from the shore. He moved closer. He wiped his glasses. He saw the raft and then he saw or thought he saw a large shape, a dark oblong form rising from the sea, a whale, a whale with open mouth about to swallow the raft. He couldn't see the woman, she had to be there but he couldn't make her out. He saw the pink mouth of the whale and rows of teeth and the huge lower jawbone shaking, or was it just the moonlight sliding over the crest of the wave? It was not a dream, it was like the impression of a dream after you wake, a mark on the inside of the eyelids.

Just at that moment the wind picked up, the waves came crashing forward onto the sandbar and turned the small craft over. Sally went into the sea. André saw the wave rise behind her, it looked like a whale opening his mouth. He saw a tail flashing above the foam, swishing from side to side, but maybe it was only the dense clouds pushed by the north wind racing across the sky. He pulled off his boots and his socks and rushed into the water. The eddy, protected by the sandbar, was deep. He swam and walked, he pushed against the waves and then he was on the sandbar, he stood up and saw the woman drifting, her body thrashing in the near wave. He swam toward her. If it was there, the whale's mouth was above him. He closed his eyes, imagining the slimy, slick, oily surface of the bottom lip. He pulled Sally toward the shore. She struggled against him. He tried to explain that he was saving her. She was confused. She tried to bite him. She pushed against him. He held on.

He kept his eyes shut tight. They were inside the whale's mouth, he felt himself sliding down, the pink tissue of the mouth, the red gums, the sharp teeth rising and falling with the sweep of the wave. He opened his eyes and saw the night sky. He was cold. He grabbed the woman, though she was bigger than he. He pulled her upward and as the mouth opened, or perhaps it was only the drift of the current, a stream of fish, weed, shell floated toward him, he pushed forward, pulling her with him, and burst out of the slimy lips that were or were not there, and in the dark water he tried to reach the shore. He couldn't do it. The waves were strong. He could feel the dark hulk of the whale drifting near. The woman had let her head lie back and she was staring at the stars. He couldn't make any headway through the waves. He was lifted up and carried downward with the

current, a riptide pulled him sideways and out. Each wave
pushed him farther away from the shore. His legs ached.
His neck was stiff. His arms were not strong. His age was
against him. He swallowed salt water and coughed. He held
on to Sally.

Leah and Ollie walked, the lighthouse at their backs,
they moved quickly, urgently. They heard the waves crashing against the shore. Their eyes scanned the water; they
walked out of range of the lighthouse. Ollie swung his
flashlight in an arc. They listened to the crash of each wave
on the shore.

Then they saw them, the man and the woman in the water
out just beyond the sandbar, lifted up in the crest of the wave,
carried back down in the returning wash of the strong riptide
that pulled them sideways and out, out toward death, instead
of in, in to home. Ollie took off his shoes, took off his jacket,
and rushed into the water. The cold bit sharply at his body. He
could see them just ahead, but when he dove under the next
wave he lost them. He called out, "Where are you, where are
you?" Water splashed in his mouth. His words disappeared
in the sea. His eyes blurred from water, he smelled sea and
weed and the wet wool of his clothes. Then he saw them
again, bobbing up and down. He thought of his body, clumsy
in the water, afraid in the dark, perhaps he couldn't reach
them, wouldn't reach them, couldn't pull them out. He
thought for an instant of Sally gone. His chest tightened. He
gasped for breath. He and Leah alone, riding a balloon high
above the dunes, waving good-bye, nothing to remind him,
nothing to hold him down, up and out, his heart beat hard. In
the empty space where Sally had been he and Leah would
plant the roots of their own life.

But his arms pulled through the water. He dove under
the next wave and moved out farther. He saw the path of the

moon on the water, running like a silver road right to his sister, right to the man who was holding his sister. His body worked. It did what it must. He shouted to André, "Here, here." André saw him and pulled Sally along. The waves went up and down, crashing finally on the shore, a clump of seaweed wound itself around Ollie's head. He tried to pull it off and was hit by the next wave. He rose up and looked for them. There they were. He was close enough to see the exhaustion on the old man's face. Sally didn't try to talk. She wanted to pat Ollie on the shoulder but his shoulder kept dipping under the water out of reach of her arm. "Follow me," he said.

He took Sally's weight from André. He moved inward now toward Leah, standing at the shore, not moving, frozen, numb with hope and its opposite. He moved slowly sideways, not directly in, the way you do with a riptide, tacking along its edges, each time coming closer to the shore. André followed behind, he heard the whoosh of a tail behind him. They crossed the sandbar. Ollie stood up and cradled his sister in his arms. He stroked her hair. She was crying, from happiness or sadness he couldn't tell. When André reached the slope of the beach and the rushing foam of the approaching waves slid against his calves, he looked back. He didn't see the whale anymore. Had it been there? He thought not. André stumbled onto the shore. Leah gave him her jacket.

Through his heavy pants Ollie could feel the cold sand, a dampness rising and cutting at his skin, a dampness from within and without. He looked up at the sky, far and cool, moon and star, darkness to the end of the world. He felt at home. "Leah," he said, "I need you."

"I know," said Leah, who was shaking still, her arms trembling from aftershock.

André was wringing the water out of his shirt, grabbing it in bunches and pulling on himself, shaking his head as if he were a dog, trying to clear his mind as well as his eyes.

"My hands hurt," said Sally.

"We can fix that," André said. It was a tone he had. It implied fixing without making any exaggerated promises. It implied that in the scheme of things, in proportion of individual to species, of space to earth, of man to God, things were not as bad as one thought. His voice carried a message that even a child of five could understand. Sally stood up and took his hand.

That night when André was in bed, a brandy in his belly, weariness in each of his bones, he curled his legs up to fit with the shape of his wife's back. He considered his life, not bad, good even. His mind turned to whales. Why did they come up to the beaches when they were ready to die? Was it possible that the whale was trying to come to Nineveh himself? With that thought he fell asleep. He woke the next morning feeling fine.

Leah called her friend Myrna.

"If Ollie hadn't been there, they both would have been carried off."

"The psychiatrist tried to save her?" said Myrna.

"Yes, he went right after her and he's not so young."

"What's his name, maybe I'll send Sheila to him."

"He might be going crazy."

"Then he's perfect for Sheila . . . Guess what I found stuffed in an empty Tampax box left right in the middle of our bed."

"What?"

"My gold bracelet, my pearls, my earrings, my pin, everything."

"A happy ending."

"For our insurance company."

"Does the bathroom still smell?"

"No," said Myrna. "We didn't find anything. We tore out the pipes in the apartment beneath us. We still didn't find anything. But it stopped. It just stopped."

"Hope it doesn't start again," said Leah.

"Oh God," said Myrna.

"We're getting married," said Leah.

"Good, good for you, good for him," said Myrna.

"Who would have thought that I would? I thought I wouldn't," said Leah.

"You're going to live happily ever after," said Myrna.

"His athlete's foot has gone away," said Leah.

"Miracle worker," said Myrna.

"We're going to move to the city. He's going to teach and I'm going back to the lab," said Leah.

"What are you going to do about his sister?" said Myrna.

"She'll get used to me. I'll get used to her," said Leah.

"Maybe she'll run away again," said Myrna.

"No," said Leah, "she won't."

"Remember, you could send her away," said Myrna.

"No," said Leah, "we couldn't."

"Why not?" said Myrna.

"She's an orphan," said Leah.

"So are you," said Myrna.

"That's something we have in common," said Leah.

The jellyfish, stirred by rough waters, were spread across the beach. The seaweed clumped together, ice forming along its rubbery stems. Out at sea, way offshore, a whale swung about, reversing direction. The currents pulled. The sandy bottom dropped sharply down into one of the fissures of the earth. Algae floated, a school of bluefish moved with purpose across the ocean's floor. A red leather glove, worn and bent, drifted with the tide.

Leah and Ollie lay together on the single bed of her child-hood home for the last time. She kissed him in the ear. He kissed her under her lips. She ran her fingers over his back. He held her breasts in his hands and swayed back and forth. "How much of love is lust?" he asked.

"How much of lust is love?" she answered. Their legs and arms hung off the edge of the bed, the quilt fell to the floor. Downstairs the weather radio continued its up-to-the-minute bulletins but nobody was listening.